POINT CRiME

THE BEAT

Black and Blue

David Belbin

D0242148

SCHOLASTIC

Scholastic Children's Books
7–9 Pratt Street, London NW1 0AE, UK
a division of Scholastic Publications Ltd
London ~ New York ~ Toronto ~ Sydney ~ Auckland

First published by Scholastic Publications Ltd, 1995

Copyright © David Belbin, 1995

ISBN 0 590 13317 9

Typeset by TW Typesetting, Midsomer Norton, Avon

Printed by Cox & Wyman Ltd, Reading, Berks.

10 9 8 7 6 5 4 3 2 1

THE BEAT

Black and Blue

Instinctively, Ruth pushed towards the officer in danger.

"My God," Clare said, pushing after her. "Do you see who that is?"

Ruth wasn't tall enough to see the officer's face. Only patches of uniform showed through the crowd.

"No," she said to her friend. "Who?"

Clare pulled Ruth through the fighting crowd. Any moment now, one of them was going to get hit. The police officer had probably been stabbed already, a terrible thought struck Ruth.

"It's not Neil, is it?" she asked Clare.

"No," Clare replied. "I'm

The city in these pages is real. The events described in them are not. All of the characters, together with the police station where some of them work, are imaginary. The author wishes to thank the many people, including serving police officers, who helped him with this series. He alone is responsible for any mistakes.

PROLOGUE

Ben took the money from the machine, crossed the road, then began to jog up the hill, thinking about his girlfriend. He would be home in ten minutes. Quick shower, then into bed. He had two days off, and wanted to be fresh tomorrow when he met Charlene off the train. He didn't see enough of her. In some ways, it was a miracle that they'd stayed together since finishing university. After all, she was in London and he was...

"There he is!"

Rapid footsteps behind him. Ben didn't look round. Being black, in this city, on a Friday night, that was provocation enough for some people. He stepped up his pace. He'd never been attacked in Nottingham. But there was always a first time. The footsteps behind him accelerated.

"Hold it right there, nigger!"

The last word made Ben tighten up inside. No one had used that word directly to him, not since he was at school. It made him want to stop, to hit out. Hard.

The sound of pounding feet grew louder. They were gaining on Ben, gaining all the time. But they wouldn't catch him. Ben knew this stretch of road better than he knew his home town. At the top of the hill he'd run into Mapperley Road, take a short cut down a dark alley. He'd be home before they sussed where he'd gone.

But Ben didn't get to the top of the hill. A white van careered across Mansfield Road, slamming on to the pavement, right in front of him. This wasn't casual, Ben realized. This was official. Which way to go? He glanced round to see how close they were.

"Gotcha!"

A white guy in an anorak rugby-tackled Ben to the ground. His mate came up from behind and landed a kick in Ben's stomach, knocking all the air out of him. Then the van door was opening and there was no point in fighting back because there were more of them in there too, only these ones were in uniform and they were dragging Ben into the van, heavy boots kicking him as they did. Then another face was in his, stripes on his shoulder. The stripes were shouting,

"We know you're not working alone. Where's your

mate? Come on, you spook, tell us now. Where's your mate?"

Ben got back enough breath to mumble:

"I don't know what you're talking about."

A fist clobbered him in the side of the face, where a mark wouldn't show. Ben flinched. It was time to end this.

"What am I supposed to have done?" he asked, through gritted teeth.

The sergeant sneered. There were beads of sweat around his ugly moustache.

"Don't take the…"

"Am I under arrest?" Ben interrupted him.

The plain clothes one who'd rugby-tackled him spoke now.

"Don't start telling us our job, scumbag. Show us your wallet."

Slowly, Ben reached into his jeans pocket.

"You lot ought to be under arrest," he said, handing the brown leather pouch to the CID man. "All of you."

"Let's take a look at your cash cards, shall we?" the cocky plain clothes one who'd called him "nigger" said.

He opened the wallet and swore. Then his tone changed.

"Look, I'm sorry, mate. Nothing personal. You were in the right place and you fitted the description, all right?"

Ben said nothing. The white guy went on, obnoxiously ingratiating.

"We'll run you home, all right?"

"What's going on?" the sergeant with the moustache wanted to know.

The guy in the anorak held out Ben's wallet so that the other three men could see the warrant card in it.

"That's right," Ben told them, not trying to hide the bitterness in his voice. "I'm a police officer."

1

Ruth was still getting to know the city on her weekends off. Clare, her best mate, who'd grown up here, had given Ruth the tour, introduced her to the night life. Clare liked this area, Hockley, with its trendy shops and film theatre, out by the old Lace Market section of the city. But Clare was back with her boyfriend these days and less available for shopping trips. Most of the clothes shops in Hockley were too expensive for Ruth anyway, except for *Wild Clothing*, which sold secondhand American stuff. She tried some on, but they didn't suit her. Ruth was too small for that fifties look, too ordinary looking.

Ruth spotted a brightly painted shop with posters in the window. A bookshop. She decided to check it out. The window display was full of black women writers: Toni Morrison, Alice Walker, Gloria Naylor – Ruth remembered Clare going on about one of her books. Which one was it? She went inside. The wall to her right was covered with posters advertising demonstrations, pressure groups and alternative therapies. A saxophone played cool jazz in the background.

Ruth drifted through the shop, checking out the different sections: Inner Being, Jewish Interest, Media Studies, Gays and Lesbians. She paused to examine the table of Bargain Books.

"Excuse me."

Ruth moved aside to let a woman in a wheelchair get past. It was then that she noticed the accommodation board, pinned to one of the pillars near the Media section. Ruth and Clare had been looking for somewhere to live for a couple of weeks now, with no luck. Ruth walked over and checked out the adverts. They were mostly for house shares, not flats. If you wanted one of them it helped to be a feminist, a vegetarian and a non-smoker. *No good*, Ruth thought. *Clare likes meat too much*. Nevertheless, she wrote down a couple of phone numbers, laughing to herself as she imagined the reaction when the landlady asked what the girls did.

"So, you're students, are you?"

"No," Ruth would say. "We're probationary police officers."

With some people, the job they did came over like a lead balloon.

Ruth was putting her pen away when she heard the noise from outside. She looked at her watch. It sounded like football supporters, but they ought to be at the match by now. She looked round the pillar just as the balding guy from behind the counter tried to block the doorway.

"I'm sorry. You can't come in here with those badges on. We have a policy which says…"

He didn't get to finish his sentence, because the next moment he was on the ground, doubled up in pain.

Then they swarmed in, more of them than Ruth could count. They filled the place, outnumbering the people in the shop by at least four to one. Behind Ruth, a woman came out of the office, took one look, and went back in. Ruth hoped that she was dialling three nines. Books began to fly through the air. Ruth saw one of them pulling the VDU from the counter, flinging it through the window. Someone screamed as the window smashed. The vandals were shouting: swear-words mostly. One of them came right up to Ruth. There was a crude boot tattooed just above his left eyebrow and Ruth thought for a moment that he was going to headbutt her. He screamed *"LESBIAN!"* so loud that it deafened her. Then he struck out, missing Ruth, but knocking the CD rack off the wall.

Ruth stepped back, into the office doorway, as the thugs charged past her in a flood of shaved heads, tattoos and denim. She could hardly make out the words they were shouting any more. It was a cacophony of swearing, singing, laughing, crashing noises, punctuated by cries of pain from customers who got in the way.

As one of them tore down the stand of political newspapers, the woman in the wheelchair yelled "*Nazi Scum!*" at them.

Ruth cringed as two of the scum knocked the wheelchair over and kicked the woman across the floor. Then they tried to lift the wheelchair and shove it through the remaining, unbroken window. But this proved to be too much for them, so they turned their venom instead on the Jewish Interest section. Not satisfied with throwing all the books out, they pulled the bookcase away from the wall, meaning to topple it on to one of the workers, who was getting up off the floor.

Then a police siren sounded outside and, moments later, they were gone, as quickly as they had come, tearing down the street like a victorious army on the rampage. As the police car parked on the street outside, Ruth looked around. The raid had lasted mere minutes, but she was standing knee deep in battered books. The shop, which had seemed so colourful and peaceful when she walked in, now looked as though an earthquake had hit it.

Five customers and three workers stood staring at each other, in a kind of daze.

Ruth realized that she was shaking. She had been, still was, afraid. Then she saw the disabled woman on the floor and went with the woman from the office to help her back into the wheelchair. As they lifted her, two police officers came through the door. There were more sirens in the street.

"Which way did they go?" one of them asked.

Someone told him. The woman in the wheelchair thanked Ruth and the young woman, assuring them that she wasn't hurt, though her clothes were torn and her face was pale as death.

An ambulance arrived. The worker who received the kicking was being helped out to it. One of the police officers came over to Ruth and the woman in the wheelchair. He began to ask questions.

"How many were there? What were they wearing? Can you describe the ones who assaulted you?"

The woman in the wheelchair shook her head. Ruth dredged her memory, trying to freeze-frame the images, but coming up with a blurred expression, filled with hate. She wished that someone would make her a cup of hot, sweet tea.

"How about you?" the officer said to Ruth. "Can you say which ones did what?"

"I'm afraid not," Ruth told him. "They all looked the same to me."

*　*　*

After they'd been to bed, Ben took a shower. When he came out, his girlfriend was staring at him, and it wasn't because he had the body of an Olympic athlete.

"Those bruises," she said. "Where did you get them?"

He told her.

"So if you hadn't been in the force, they'd have beaten you up more?"

"That's about the size of it," Ben agreed.

Charlene shook her head.

"I don't understand how you can stay in the job. There are a hundred other things you could do. What are you trying to prove?"

"If I packed it in," Ben told her, as he dried himself off, "then I'd have let them drive me out, first aggro I got. What would that prove?"

"It wouldn't prove anything," Charly told him, stroking his bruised thigh. "What I'm trying to say is … this isn't about proving things. This is about you being happy … you and me being happy, too."

"I like my job," Ben replied. "So, all right, those guys were well out of line. Maybe they'll think a bit harder before they jump the next suspect who just happens to be black."

"Who are you trying to fool?" Charly asked him.

Ben shrugged. Charly and he went back years, but they still differed in how to deal with racism.

Charly believed in direct confrontation, every time. Ben varied his approach according to the circumstances. Sometimes you needed to be diplomatic, to defuse the situation with humour.

"You're going to put a complaint in?"

It sounded like a question but it wasn't. As far as Charly was concerned, it was a statement of his moral obligation.

"I don't know," Ben said, putting on a soft, white shirt. "I don't think so. They were on a case. I fitted the description. They had a right to stop me."

Charlene's voice became sarcastic.

"That's right, Uncle Tom, and they had a right to beat you up, too, I suppose? In fact, I guess you asked for it."

Ben sighed.

"A couple of them kicked me. One punched me in the face. I wasn't beaten up. Let's not argue about this. I'm sorry that I even told you about it."

Their eyes met. Both of them sensed that, if they continued this argument, neither one of them would back down. They'd been together long enough to know when to walk away from a row.

Time together was precious. Since finishing university, eighteen months before, Ben and Charly were lucky if they saw each other one weekend in three. Charlene was training to be a solicitor, Ben a police officer. Neither career left much space for a social life outside the job. You had to make allowances. Ben handed Charlene her long dress and she slipped it on.

"I've got an interview," she said, more affectionately. "In Nottingham. Good firm. Bit traditional, maybe, but they do a fair bit of legal aid work."

"For the sort of people I arrest," Ben said, hoping she realized he meant it as a joke. Charly smiled.

"Yeah, that's right," she said. "We'd be a team. You arrest 'em. I defend 'em. It's a living."

"Making crime pay," Ben suggested, with a smile in his voice.

Later, they were standing by the Mansfield Road waiting for a bus. They were going to see Ben's parents for the afternoon.

"What case were they on, anyway?" Charly asked.

"Who?"

Ben knew what she meant, and was sorry that she'd brought it up again.

"The cops who beat you up last night."

"It was a kind of stake-out," Ben told her. "They explained it to me. They think that there's some kind of team, moving from city to city, doing cash-point machines. I'd just taken fifty quid out of a machine which had a hundred quid taken from it a few moments before, using a card which was reported stolen."

Charly wasn't convinced.

"How did they know it was stolen?"

"They had someone inside the bank, checking every withdrawal against a database. But they weren't coordinated enough. They saw me leaving and assumed I was the one, when in fact it was the guy before me, some insignificant-looking bloke in a raincoat."

Someone else arrived at the bus stop and Ben stopped talking about it. You didn't discuss the job in public places, even though this particular case wasn't his job, but someone else's.

"You're sure now?" Charly teased him. "Or am I secretly going out with a bank robber?"

"Put it this way, Charly, I hope you've got the right change for the bus, because I've only got enough for me."

It was a toss-up, which of them had the least money. Both were still in debt from university. Charly earned more than Ben did, but, then, living in London was much more expensive than living in Nottingham.

Charly asked after Ben's parents.

"Are they still talking about going back to Jamaica?"

He shook his head.

"Not since Christmas. It's always the same at Christmas. They think they'll go back when they've both retired, but you know Dad – they'll have to carry him out of his bus feet first."

*   *   *

"And would you recognize any of them again?"

"Maybe the first one," Ruth said. "The one who knocked the guy over. After that it was all a blur. What are the chances?"

The CID bloke made an empty gesture with his hands.

"You know the score. It all hinges on identification. We stopped the bus they got on. They're on their way to cells at Division now."

"What were they?" Ruth asked. "On some kind of smash–up–a–city awayday?"

"Near enough," the officer told her. "They were going to London for a rally when they got word of a court order, banning it. So they decided to look for fun a little nearer to home."

"I see."

"Could you come down to Division in a couple of hours, see if you recognize them? You'd make a good witness."

"Well, I guess…"

The bloke looked embarrassed.

"I know it's Saturday night and all that. You're probably going out somewhere. If you want to leave it…"

"No, it's all right," Ruth told him. "I've got nothing on. I'd like to help nail them, all of them."

"That might not be too easy," Ruth was told. "Shall we send a car for you?"

"I've got my own, thanks."

"About seven, then. OK?"

"OK."

It was a mild January afternoon. Ruth decided to walk across town back to her bedsit. The room was a waste of money, really, while she was doing her training. She'd be better off going home, if it wasn't such a long drive. But she'd needed somewhere to live during her two six-week patrols in Nottingham, and home was a bunch of bad memories to her. She'd rather spend her weekends alone.

Her flat was cold and dusty. Ruth sneezed as she turned on the two bar electric fire and huddled down in front of it. She switched on the TV. The raid on the bookshop had made the local evening news. Ruth looked at the pictures. It was funny. She felt more frightened thinking about it now than she had done at the time. She turned over and watched *Blind Date*, instead, trying not to think about her love-life, or lack of one. Then she got changed. Maybe she'd take in a film at the Showcase, the multiplex which was on the way back from Division. Anything was better than another Saturday night in on her own.

2

Some days are longer than others. The really exciting ones – like today – hurtle by so fast you wish you could slow them down, savour them. Jed sat in the police cell, trying to figure out how he would describe the day when he got home. He thought about how it would make him sound. *The bookshop raid? Yeah, I was in on that. You should of been there, should of seen the looks on their faces as we gutted the place.* But he mustn't say anything here. When the police ask you questions, you keep your trap shut. Some of them might be all right, share his point of view, but you never knew which ones to trust.

There was someone coming down the corridor now. Jed hoped it was the solicitor. He wanted to get out of here. The rest of the lads were dead confident, said they'd be home by closing time. Jed felt like a drink now, though he wasn't old enough to have one in a pub. But suppose it didn't go so smoothly? He'd never been arrested before. How long could they keep you before they charged you?

It wasn't the brief. It was a young woman: short, smart looking. Jed thought he knew her. She'd been wearing a duffle-coat before, looked scruffier. But it was her, the one from the bookshop. Now she was peering into the cells, taking a good look. Seeing her face, a bunch of the lads began making monkey noises, suggesting things they'd like her to do to them. The girl didn't react. Jed admired her cool. She wasn't bad looking, now she had decent clothes on.

Jed was in the last cell, on his own, because he was a juvenile. The girl took a long, hard look at him, then walked off with the custody officer. Jed shivered, though it wasn't cold, not very. He needed to get out of here soon, while he still had plenty of bottle. He hoped that the brief would come soon.

"Ring any bells?"

Ruth's reply was apologetic.

"I recognized that last one, but he didn't hit me or anything. I remember thinking that he looked younger than the rest. Most of them are in their twenties, aren't they?"

"Yes. The young one, Sutcliffe, he's only seventeen. Did you see him do anything?"

"Not exactly. I mean, I guess that he was throwing books – they all were. But I didn't see him assaulting anyone, if that's what you mean."

The officer looked unhappy.

"It's going to be hard to make any but the mildest charges stick. Our only chance of making an assault charge stick is if someone IDs one of them for a specific offence."

The custody officer leant in.

"Sarge, their brief's here: Jagger."

The sergeant rolled his eyeballs.

"You know," he said to Ruth. "When we arrested these guys, they had a bunch of lists in the bus: bookshops, mosques, Anti-Nazi activists ... oh, and a bunch of 'sympathetic' lawyers, who'd represent them if they ran into any trouble. Have you heard of Jagger?"

Ruth shook her head.

"I was surprised to find him on it. Big in the Rotary club, he is. A pillar of society. Got an MBE too. This is him now."

The man who walked into the Parade room was heavily built. His suit was of an old-fashioned, double-breasted cut with shiny elbows. Its wearer had thinning black hair – dyed, Ruth thought – with even darker, curly hedges of eyebrows. His face was lined, puffy, but there was something about him, a real presence, which had to come from his eyes, which were also dark. They shone in a sharp, metallic way. He hadn't spoken, but Ruth already found him intimidating.

"You've had a bit of bother," the lawyer said, quite casually. "What are the charges?"

"No one's been charged yet," the custody officer told him. "Affray, most likely, in the first instance."

Jagger nodded in a way which indicated that he was in total agreement.

"We'd better sort something out then."

"You'll have to speak to the superintendent, sir."

"Give him a bell for me, would you?"

"Don't you want to see your clients first?"

Jagger raised one of his bushy eyebrows.

"Not particularly."

He smiled, acknowledging Ruth for the first time.

"I represent these people, but I don't like dealing with them any more than you do. They're repugnant, but they have rights, as I'm sure you're aware. I'll see them when I've sorted out bail."

"One of them's a juvenile," the custody officer told him.

"Record?"

"No."

"Then doubtless you'll be sending him home with a caution when he's had time to cool his heels."

As the custody officer tried to raise the superintendent on the phone, Ruth took her leave. She didn't like the solicitor. Yet what he said was true: even the creepiest confessed serial killer had rights. As a police officer, you had to treat all offenders with respect, no matter what your personal beliefs.

Ruth drove to the Showcase. It took her twenty minutes to get in and park, then she couldn't find one film on any of the ten screens which she wanted to watch. But she'd come this far, so she settled for a light, romantic comedy which frittered away ninety minutes of her time. As she was leaving, she spotted someone she knew in the foyer: a tall, handsome black guy.

"Ben. Hi."

"Hello, eh…"

He couldn't remember her name. Hardly surprising. They'd only been introduced once.

"What have you been to see?" she asked him.

He told her. The new Spike Lee. Ruth wished she'd gone to it too. Ben was on his own. And he was gorgeous. Ruth checked her watch.

"Got time for a quick drink?"

Ben looked a little embarrassed.

"Actually, we were going to catch the last bus."

Ruth clocked that "we". So he wasn't at the pictures on his own after all. Worse, he now knew that she was. Doubly embarrassing. As they stood there wondering what to say next, a tall black woman in a long green coat walked out of the Ladies.

"Charlene, this is Ruth. Friend of Clare's."

"Right."

The tall woman had a posh, professional accent which made Ruth conscious of her soft Yorkshire vowels. But she brazened it out.

"Where do you two live?" she asked.

"Mapperley Park," Ben told her.

"He does. I'm just visiting," Charlene explained.

"It's on my way. I'll give you a lift."

"No, really," Ben said. "There's no need to trouble."

Ruth pointed out of the window.

"Last bus is leaving. C'mon."

"It's very kind of you," Charlene said, graciously.

Of course, Mapperley Park wasn't on her way home. And she could understand why Ben couldn't afford a car, living in a posh part of town like that. She cracked a joke about it.

"I like to live near the city centre," he said. "And it's on the bus route to Mansfield."

"Why would you want to go to Mansfield?"

"It's where my family lives."

That surprised her. Ruth told them about the racists they'd picked up today. Half of them were from Mansfield. Then Charlene told Ruth that Ben had been beaten up the night before.

"In Mansfield?"

"No, on the Mansfield Road."

"By skinheads?"

"Hardly. Get this. By *police officers*."

Ruth tried to prise some more details from Ben, but he seemed embarrassed by it, so she changed the subject. When she dropped them off, Ben invited her in for coffee.

"That's nice of you but … three's a crowd. I'm going to have an early night."

"OK. Well, thanks again," Ben told her. "See you around."

I certainly hope so, Ruth thought, as she drove back to her cold, empty bedsit.

"Sorry to keep you waiting," Mr Jagger said.

That was rich: this oily toff, with the deep, snobby voice, apologizing to him.

"Are they going to let the others out?" he asked, as the solicitor led him into the station's reception area.

"Yes," Jagger told him, "in a while. On police bail. I've been organizing a couple of vans to take them home."

"What about me?" Jed asked.

"You don't need bail. The police will require you to attend your local station, where they will administer a formal caution. You may have to give evidence in court, though I doubt it."

Jed nodded. Cautions, court, it was all a load of cobblers. The police didn't know how to get serious.

He followed Jagger out into the car park.

"What I meant was, how am I going to get home?"

"Ah, yes. I've been trying to reach your mother, but with no success."

"She'll be in the pub."

"And your father's not around?"

Jed stared at the tarmacked ground.

"That's none of your business."

Jagger ignored Jed's rudeness.

"Anyway, I persuaded the police to release you to me. I'll run you home."

"To Mansfield? I don't mind waiting for the others, save you time."

"It won't take long," Jagger purred, as they reached the far end of the car park. The solicitor wasn't kidding. He unlocked the door of a sleek, vintage car, a Jaguar SV 12. Inside, it smelt of money, a combination of old leather and new cigar smoke. Soon, they were tearing down dark, empty lanes to the north of the county. As he drove, Jagger talked. Jed was expecting a lecture, but that wasn't what he got.

"The police tell me that you haven't been in trouble before. Not done anything, or not been caught?"

Jagger's was a big voice, the kind you didn't tell lies to.

"Not been caught," Jed admitted.

"I thought so. You're lucky. It's hard to make your way in the world if you have a criminal record."

"If you say so."

"I take it you don't have a job?"

The car was doing over a hundred now. Jagger didn't take his eyes off the dark, frosty road. Nevertheless, Jed felt like the lawyer was burrowing into his soul. He had to be very careful what he said.

"What's a job?" he asked, cynically.

Jagger gave a short, humourless laugh.

"You strike me as an intelligent lad. You have principles, which I admire, even if some of them seem misguided…"

So it *was* turning into a lecture, after all. Jagger paused.

"If you can stay out of trouble, I might be able to find some work for you."

Jed waited for the catch, but Jagger wasn't telling him anything else.

"Interested?" the lawyer asked, after a few seconds.

Jed didn't hesitate.

"Tell me more," he said.

3

Monday was a rest day for Neil's shift. The week began on Tuesday morning, at five to six, in the parade room. Tim Cooper was telling a story.

"There was this bank right by the Victoria Centre which had a night safe – you know, one of those big letter-box jobs. A lot of the market traders would use it, especially on a Saturday, because they didn't like to take a lot of readies home.

"So, this particular Saturday, there was a notice covering up the slot: *Temporarily out of order. Please use Security Guard*. And there's this bloke with a helmet and a uniform standing by the safe. And everybody hands him their money. End of the day he scarpers, taking ten grand with him. The perfect crime."

Everyone laughed.

"They never caught him?" Neil asked, not sure if the story was true or not.

"Nope," Tim told him. "Want to know my theory? I think it was Ben here."

Another round of laughter.

"What's the joke?" Neil asked Ben, who was his partner.

Ben told him. The two men hadn't seen each other since Neil came off shift on Friday.

"You're not putting in a complaint?" Neil asked, when Ben had finished.

"Would you?"

"If I got a kicking, sure. They were well out of order."

"They apologized," Ben told him.

"And that made it all right, did it?"

Ben shrugged.

"This way, if I come up against any of those guys again, they owe me. The other way, I'm the coon that got them into trouble. It wasn't a hard choice." Neil flinched. Words like "coon" make him uncomfortable, even when they were used by someone black. Every other kid at his school had been black, or Asian. You didn't use words like that around them, not if you had an ounce of respect.

Before they could finish the conversation, Inspector Grace came in. The inspector, only a few years older than Neil, was in charge of five shifts, including this one. He was a high flyer, and, Neil thought, suspiciously slimy.

"You've got a new shift sergeant," Grace announced, as the parade began. The shift sergeant actually ran the shift, deciding what each of the six to eight people on it should be doing. Everyone looked around, expecting someone to walk into the room. Then Jan Hunt, who was sitting in front of the bulletin board, gave a small wave.

Neil smiled. Jan had been the shift sergeant for a few months before she went off on maternity leave last year. She had also been his mentor, or tutor, while he was a probationer. When Jan returned after having her baby, Henry, she had been assigned to their shift on a temporary basis. Now that Bill Cope had retired, she was permanent, or as permanent as anyone ever was in this job.

There was a round of congratulations, then Jan got down to business.

"We're really short-staffed at the moment. Mike's sick leave has been extended and we won't have Clare back from Ryton for a couple of months..." Clare Coppola was Neil's girlfriend. "Therefore, I've asked Division to assign us two more officers for now."

"Three cheers for the sarge," John Farraday said, without irony.

"Not a snowball in hell's chance," Tim Cooper told the parade.

"I thought," Jan continued, "that we'd be lucky to get one officer, but – believe it or not, Tim – they're giving us two. I want you to partner Carl Price."

Carl Price. Neil knew that name well. He was the officer at West Bridgford who had originally been Clare's tutor officer, but they hadn't got on. Clare had avoided giving Neil many details, but the phrase "sexual harassment" had come up. Now, as if on cue, Price walked into the room, a large-faced, grinning copper, with short black hair, a couple of years older than Neil.

"And John, I'd like you to go on the beat with Baljit Singh."

John turned his lip up. He and Tim were usually partnered together, but he knew better than to complain at the new sarge's first parade.

"One of our Asian brothers, eh…"

Now Inspector Grace spoke.

"I think it'll be particularly good for us to have an Asian officer in such a visible role. Be sure you make him welcome."

Grace spoke again.

"Actually, I'm not just here to introduce Jan. I also want to inform you about something which is going on. CID have been on to this since last Thursday, but they only bothered to inform us when they accidentally picked up one of our officers as he came home from work on Friday night."

Everyone looked at Ben. He joined in the laughter.

"Cash machines," Grace went on. "There's a scam going on but no one's sure what it is…"

He was interrupted by the arrival of an officer in a turban.

"PC Singh, please sit down."

John Farraday introduced everybody. Neil remembered Baljit. They'd been at Ryton together. He wondered why he'd got a transfer.

"As I was saying," Grace went on. "We've got a bit of a mystery. Have you heard the phrase 'phantom withdrawals'?"

Baljit raised a hand, like a schoolboy in a classroom.

"Money disappearing from a cashpoint machine," he said. "The card owner claims not to have had their card stolen, but not to have withdrawn the money themselves. It's meant to amount to millions a year."

"Quite right," Grace said. "And that's only the figure reported. It's possible that tens of millions disappear without the bank account holders actually noticing. How many of you keep a complete list of all your withdrawals?"

No one responded. Grace continued.

"This is a crime which is very hard to pin down. We've all come across the situation where someone is mugged or kidnapped, and forced to reveal his cash card number to his attacker, but, with phantom withdrawals, there's no proof that the crime even took place."

"How do they do it?" Tim Cooper asked.

"That's what CID are investigating. Ah, you're just in time."

A tall man in his late thirties walked into the room. He was in plain clothes but you'd never have mistaken him for a civilian.

"This is Inspector Greasby. CID. He'll carry on this briefing."

"Initially, the banks insisted that there was no such thing as a phantom withdrawal," the inspector began. "They argued that it was a con – friends or relatives were using the victims' cards to make withdrawals without their knowledge. Therefore it was the victims' fault for letting their Personal Identification Number be known to other people. But they had to back down when an ATM service engineer for the Clydesdale Bank admitted stealing £17,000 over two years using fake cards that he'd made.

"There are eighty million cards in circulation – at least two per adult – and there are three hundred thousand electric terminals which will take them. This kind of crime is big and getting enormous, but, so far, we've done little about it, preferring to concentrate on stolen and bogus credit cards.

"You see, it's often hard to pinpoint how the money's gone, which makes this kind of crime very hard to prove. There are five ways that we know of:

1. The cards are stolen in transit.
2. The cards are lost, stolen or borrowed.
3. The thief gets hold of the card's PIN number, then has it encoded on a fake card.
4. Machine malfunction.
5. Fraud within the bank itself.

"The operation which began this weekend is a stake-out. We're targetting machines where dodgy withdrawals are taking place, and trying to catch fraudsters in the act. Trouble is, you can't always tell when a crime's being committed until a long time afterwards. So cameras have been installed in the machines they're targetting."

Greasby held out a photograph of a nondescript looking man in a hat and a raincoat.

"This is the chap who they should have arrested when they picked you up, Ben. The card he used had been reported lost in the post. But by the time the computer had got this information and relayed it to the boys hiding in the transit van, chummy here had scarpered."

Ben smiled ruefully. Neil knew that look. His partner wished that this story would hurry up and go away.

Greasby produced two more photographs. Both were of youngish men.

"So far, these three have been photographed using stolen cards. We don't know if they're connected with each other. Anyone recognize any of them?"

The photographs were passed around. Heads were shaken.

"All I'm saying is: be aware of this investigation; be on the look-out for these men; and if you run up against any of our officers investigating this case, be as cooperative as you can. That's all."

The CID man left. Everyone was getting up to go about their business when Inspector Grace came over to Neil and Ben.

"Ben, I'd like a word."

Ben glanced at Neil.

"I'll go and sort out the car," Neil told him.

For once, Jan had everybody out but herself. She had some paperwork to dispose of and a court appearance later. It felt good to have a full section, even if it was only temporary.

"See you, Ben."

"Yes, sir."

She'd forgotten that Paul Grace was still in his office.

"Got a minute, Jan?"

"Of course, sir."

She assumed that he wanted to talk to her about the cashpoint thing. She was wrong.

"Good officer, Shipman."

Alarm bells rang in Jan's head. She had been

Ben's tutor officer for a while, but they hadn't got on. Grace continued.

"Ben's not taking the events of Friday night any further. I thought you ought to know."

"I wouldn't have blamed him if he had," Jan said, cautiously.

"No. Nor would I."

Race was a hot issue in the force these days. When Jan first joined, Notts had a bad reputation for racism. There was a lot of publicity. You had to watch your words. Grace went on.

"Your newest recruit, Baljit: he had a pretty tough time out in the sticks."

Jan read between the lines.

"I'll make sure he's treated fairly, sir."

"I don't doubt that for a moment, Jan. I'd like you to do a bit more. Watch his back."

"Is there something I should know about him, sir?"

Grace thought for a moment.

"Baljit nearly failed his probation, put in a complaint about … a superior. He's a good officer, I'm sure. He had every right to make a complaint, but…"

"We don't want to give him any grounds to make another one."

"Right. And while we're on the subject, have you seen this?"

He held out the weekly orders. One of the items

pointed out that there was a place available on a racial awareness course to be held the weekend after next.

"A course like that would look very good on your CV," Grace told her.

Jan tried not to squirm.

"I'm sure it would, sir, but, as you know, I have a young child…"

Grace interrupted her.

"We've got two officers from ethnic minorities on this shift now. That's unusual."

Jan sensed a hidden agenda.

"Are you telling me that I might get to keep Baljit on my shift?"

"If his face fits. I realize it's short notice, but I'm sure you'll agree an understanding of ethnic minority issues is an essential part of your job."

This isn't a request, Jan thought. It's an order.

"Would you think about it? Let me know by the end of the shift and I'll see if I can get you that place."

"Sir."

The inspector left. It was a double edged thing, Jan realized. Go on the course, and she might get to keep an extra officer. Don't go, and Grace would keep reminding her that she had dumped on her black trainee PC at the first opportunity. She thought about it. Could she get childcare? What would Kevin, her husband, have to say? They'd missed Sunday dinner at his mother's once this month already. All this hassle for a stupid course.

Race awareness. Who needed it?

"You're lucky that Mr Jagger's taken an interest in you," the youth worker told Jed. "There are tons of kids your age out of work on this estate. Unemployment here's over fifty per cent. That's why this club's so important."

Jed mumbled something, trying not to sound too surly. It was only a government training scheme. The pay was lousy. That was probably why none of the kids on the estate wanted to work here. But Jagger had promised that there would be prospects for him. It was better than what he could get up to in Mansfield.

"Start by taking down any of the notices on the board which are out of date, would you?"

The youth worker gave Jed a look which implied that he doubted whether Jed could read. Jed ignored it. Appearances weren't everything. He might have his hair really short and heavy boots, but his GCSEs were pretty good. The careers officer had tried to persuade him to go to sixth form college. But Jed had other ideas.

The notices on the board were mostly boring, trivial: welfare advice, safe sex education, local councillor's surgeries. There was one for an ethnic arts festival. Jed tore that down, even though the festival hadn't happened yet. This estate was practically all white, and a lot of people wanted it to stay that way. He rearranged the posters so that the gap left wasn't obvious. Then he added one of his own to the display.

**WHITE REVOLUTION IS
THE ONLY SOLUTION!**

If anyone accused him of putting it up, he'd deny it, say the thing was there already and what was wrong with it, anyway? Stupidity was a good disguise. People took one look at him and thought: thick as a brick. But they'd have to think again when the brick was coming through their window.

4

The week passed quickly. Neil liked being on mornings. You got the rest of the day to yourself, which allowed plenty of time for househunting. Neil had saved enough for a deposit. Now it was a case of finding the right place. This weekend, Clare had agreed to go with him to visit a small semi in Carrington. He'd already seen it once and liked it. Now he was picking Clare up from her parents' home, which was itself for sale. Maria Coppola answered the door.

"Neil, come in. You know Clare. She's only just got up. But she says she'll be down in a minute."

Neil accepted a cup of tea and one of Mrs Coppola's poppy seed cakes. Despite her name, Maria Coppola wasn't Italian. She was born and bred in Nottingham, like her daughter. But her husband, Nick, had moved here from near Naples when he was young. Neil asked after him.

"He's on a job."

"Busy?"

Nick Coppola ran a small building firm.

"Work's picking up a bit, but it's not steady, so Nick isn't hiring. He's putting in a lot of extra hours himself instead."

"Had much interest in the house?"

Maria shook her head.

"Two couples in three months. It's a buyer's market. You ought to be able to get a bargain. Ah, here she is."

Clare was only wearing jeans and a dark sweater, but she looked like a film star to Neil. He was still as smitten with Clare as when he first met her, but tried not to let it show too much. Their relationship was as on-off as his football team's chances. One season, County were pressing for promotion, the next, staring relegation in the face.

"Are you ready? We're meant to be there at twelve."

"They'll wait. Let me drink half a coffee first."

Once they were in the car, Neil asked Clare about her week at Ryton. She was on Mod seven, which meant that she was doing her driving course.

"I'm thinking of buying a car," she told Neil. "Ruth says I'm stupid, that when we get a flat together, I can share hers – she'll put me on the insurance – and you've got a car too, of course. But I think I'd feel more independent if I had my own car. What do you think?"

Neil considered. He liked it when Clare asked him for his opinion.

"It's a lot of money," he said. "Not just buying a car, but the insurance. I've got this registered under my mum's name, but when I leave home…"

He finished the sentence with an expansive shrug. Clare nodded. Neil liked his girlfriend relying on him for lifts, but didn't mention this. They arrived at the house. It was a modern two up, two down, on a small estate near Carrington, just off his beat. The couple who owned the place had moved for career reasons and it had been standing empty for a while. The price was near the top of Neil's range, but it was good value, as the estate agent kept pointing out while she showed them around.

"What do you think?" Neil asked Clare, when they were finally left alone in the fitted kitchen.

"It's nice," Clare said. "I like the area. It's quiet, good for the shops. Maybe you should go for it."

Neil thought that he heard some kind of doubt in her voice. He wanted Clare to love his house, not just think that it was nice. One day, he hoped, she would live in it with him.

"But…" he said.

"What do you mean, *but*?"

"There was a 'but' in your voice."

Clare shrugged.

"If it was me," she said, "I'd want somewhere older, with more character. The rooms in here are a bit small, a bit square. But it's ideal for *you*: compact, convenient, easy to heat and clean. I could really see it suiting you down to the ground."

They fell into silence. The estate agent re-emerged.

"Are you ready to make an offer?" she asked, hopefully.

"I'll have to think about it some more," Neil told her, knowing he'd say "no", that Clare's opinion counted for more than his own. "I'll let you know."

"Did you hear about what happened in the book-shop last week?" Clare asked Neil when they were back in the car, going down the Hucknall Road.

"I did."

"Do you think it was a one-off or the beginning of something?"

Neil wasn't interested in the bookshop.

"It was just a load of cloth-heads from the sticks putting the wind up a bunch of hippies."

"*Hippies?* You're so narrow-minded sometimes. Are you saying that Ruth's a hippy? What's wrong with...?"

Neil saw something and interrupted her.

"Hold on."

They were stopped at the traffic lights.

"What is it?" Clare said.

"That guy, at the cashpoint machine over there."

"Is he wanted or something?"

The man Neil had seen looked like one of the pictures which Inspector Grace had shown them on Tuesday. He was nondescript, slightly shabby. And he wore a hat. Not the same one as on the photo, but … there was something furtive about the way he stood over the machine, waiting. Neil tried to decide what to do. Ahead of him, the lights changed. The man at the machine withdrew his card, pocketed the money, then set off in the opposite direction from Neil, up the hill. Neil hadn't got a proper look at him. Behind them, cars were hooting.

"Do you want me to get out and follow him?" Clare asked.

That was Clare for you, jumping in where angels feared to tread. Neil put his foot on the accelerator.

"Probably my imagination," he said, making a mental note to check with CID whether there had been a bogus withdrawal from that machine today. He didn't want to involve Clare in this. Sometimes he felt like their entire relationship was consumed by police work.

"Where do you want to go?" he asked her.

"I told Ruth we might pick her up and take her to Rufford Park if the weather was nice. What do you think?"

Neil thought that Ruth ought to spend her weekends at home with her parents. Didn't she see Clare all week at Ryton? He wanted to see his girlfriend on her own. But he didn't say any of this.

"Why not?" he replied, cheerfully. "Rufford it is."

Originally, Ben planned to join Charly in London for the weekend, but she rang him on Thursday night to say that something had come up. He was at a loose end. He had only been in the city for a few months, and hadn't really made any new friends outside the job. He rang a couple of mates in Mansfield and arranged to meet them for a drink. He would have dinner with his parents and sleep at home tonight.

Mansfield bus station always depressed Ben. Walking through it in the grey afternoon, he noted two new "BNP" logos crudely spray-painted on the metal shelters. Someone had written "blacks go home" beneath the timetable by the entrance. For Ben, this *was* home. He and his two sisters had been born in this town. He could never understand why his parents left Jamaica to come here, of all places. They knew someone who knew someone. That was reason enough, then.

Mansfield wasn't as racist a place as the graffiti indicated. In twenty-one years he had not been beaten up, or even chased, because of his colour, as he had been in Nottingham the Friday before last. But there were certain areas and certain pubs it was best to avoid if you were black. If you did go into them, you had to make sure that you were with someone who was known there, someone who would stand up for you if there was trouble. Round here, if you were black, you were noticed. Twenty years ago there were twenty black families in Mansfield. Now there were forty. It wasn't a lot.

Ben's sisters had both left home. Diane, who was older than him, was a primary teacher in Rotherham. Alice, the youngest, was training to be a nurse in Nottingham. His mother was a nurse, too, although she'd had to retire recently because of back trouble. His father still drove buses.

Ben always liked to bring something for his parents: a video, some chocolates, a bottle of wine. Today, he realized, he had nothing. Usually, these days, it was Charly who chose the gift, but her absence was no reason for him to forget. Ben stopped at the shop on the corner of his street. Mum always called it the "Paki" shop, much to her children's annoyance. Apart from the word's racist overtones, the shop's owners weren't from Pakistan. They were Ugandan Asians.

One of the owners, Mr Hanspal, greeted him.

"How's the city treating you, Ben?"

"Can't complain, Jatinder. How's business?"

Jatinder shrugged.

"No better, no worse. We're scraping around in the bottom of the barrel, same as everyone else. Since the mines closed…"

He paused. There was a noise outside.

"Quick!" Jatinder urged. "Get down!"

Ben did as he was told, though he had no idea why. There was a loud *thud*, followed by the sound of swearing outside. Whatever they'd thrown had bounced off the window.

"Reinforced plastic," Jatinder told Ben.

Jatinder hurried to the door to lock it, but he was too late. Three youths pushed their way in. They had flimsy football scarves round the lower part of their faces. Ben's instinct was to arrest them. Had they committed an offence yet, he wondered. Did a brick bouncing off a window count?

"Take this, Paki!"

The newspaper which they threw across the counter was filled with dog faeces. Ben tried to grab one of the lads. All he got was the scarf. The lad was younger than he'd expected. Then the one who'd thrown the newspaper pulled a knife from an inside pocket.

"Want some?"

Ben backed off and the boys were gone, running up the street, laughing. Ben and Jatinder looked at each other.

"Where's your phone?" Ben asked.

The place stank. Already, Jatinder was moving

the soiled papers from the counter, calling his wife to bring the mop and bucket.

"To call the police? Forget it. Waste of time."

"We saw the face of one of them. I could identify him."

"Sure," Jatinder said. "He goes to court, gets a fine. The next week, my shop is burnt down. Something like this happens every few months. I can live with it, Ben. I'm only glad that I replaced the glass the last time that they smashed the windows."

"But, but..." Ben found himself spluttering, "they're criminals ... cowardly little thugs. You can't let them get away with..."

Jatinder pointed at the newspaper full of excrement.

"You think this is bad? I know people who've had these packages soaked in petrol, set alight and exploded over their living-rooms."

"So you'll wait until they do that before you complain?" Ben challenged. Jatinder shook his head. He explained patiently as he cleaned the counter.

"How old were those lads – sixteen, seventeen? There's nothing for them round here, no hope of work. They see a bloke in a turban with what looks to them like a successful business – of course they resent it. They need education, not punishment."

"That doesn't justify..."

"Justify, justify ... the world isn't a just place, Ben. Here."

He handed Ben the box of chocolates he had come in for.

"Pay me later. I need to blast this place with air freshener now."

Ben let himself be ushered out of the shop. He couldn't believe that he hadn't called the police. It went against the grain. But if Jatinder didn't want to...

Ben walked down the street to his parents' house, remembering the young racist who had threatened him with a pocket knife. Ben cursed his own cowardice, or discretion, or defeat, call it what you will. Perhaps Jatinder was right. Perhaps turning the other cheek was better for the soul than retaliation. But you couldn't be philosophical all the time. If you didn't resist, the next time they came, one of them might use his knife, or worse...

Ben knocked on the door of his parents' house and tried to act like nothing had happened.

5

Neil stood in the inspector's office, repeating what he had seen on Saturday.

"You *saw* him and did nothing about it?"

Grace's voice was angry. Neil tried to keep calm.

"He matched a vague description, sir. I didn't get a good look at him."

"Good enough to realize that he resembled the photograph, though."

"Yes, sir."

Neil hoped that this rollocking wouldn't last too long.

"Weren't you telling me the other day that you hope eventually to transfer to CID, PC Foster?"

"Yes, sir."

"Then you've got a funny way of going about it."

It emerged that money had been stolen from the machine, using a card which its owner claimed never to have received.

"He reported it missing, which is why the computer says this was a fraudulent transaction, but it is possible that the card owner – one Ray Willow – is trying a little confidence trick," Grace told Neil and Ben.

"You mean, pretending that it hasn't turned up, then using it to rob himself?"

"Precisely. It's an increasingly common crime. But your seeing the man in the raincoat means that the cardholder is probably kosher. Still, we'd like you to see this Mr Willow."

"Why me?" Neil asked. "What about CID?"

"CID are short-staffed. Also, you saw a man using a card at about the right time. We need to know if it could have been the cardholder. Anyway, he lives on your beat."

"Beat? I thought we were in a car?"

"You were. But all good things must come to an end. Jan wants your car today, I believe. And I want you out walking. Keep your eye on any cash machines you pass, won't you?"

"Yes, sir."

"Is this some kind of punishment?" Ben asked, as they trudged through the Meadows.

Neil apologized. He didn't mind being out

walking in the summer, but in the winter, it was bad news. The press and parliament were always going on about getting more coppers on the beat: a nonsense, as far as he was concerned. Beat coppers were only effective if they were always on at the same time, preferably seven days a week. That way, they got to know an area and the area got to know and trust them. It was called community policing. But to do it effectively required huge staffing levels. No one was willing to pay that kind of money.

The station had a couple of community police officers working regular weekday hours. But that was as far as it went. In any shift, there would usually be two officers out walking the beat, providing something important didn't get in the way. But because of the shift system, it was rarely the same two officers at the same time, so the community didn't get to know the coppers and the coppers didn't get to know the community.

Neil and Ben reached the house of the man with the "stolen" card. One look at him and Neil knew that he wasn't the bloke he'd seen on Saturday. This guy was shorter and much older. Yet he could have lied about the card not arriving, got someone else to draw the money out for him.

"Have the bank recredited my account yet?" Mr Willow wanted to know.

"I'm afraid that's nothing to do with us," Neil explained. "I expect that they will do in due course."

"Because I've heard that banks can get stroppy about this sort of thing."

"I wouldn't worry about it," Neil assured him. "We just need to ask you a few questions."

Ray Willow lived in a nice, semi-detached house on a tree-lined street. Not bad, for a single, part time music teacher, which was what he claimed to be. But you could never tell with people and money. He could be a drug dealer, or a bank robber, or a very highly paid musician. Or he could have inherited it, or bought the house cheaply years and years ago. It was best not to have too many pre-conceptions in this job. Better to go on evidence, and instinct. Was this guy telling the truth? Neil couldn't say.

"Could anyone else have picked up your card and PIN number?"

"Hardly. I live alone."

"You don't have a cleaner, or friends to stay…"

"No."

"You've not had a burglary recently?"

"I'd have reported it, wouldn't I? The two things are posted separately, you know. The number arrived, but the card never did. The bank said there should be a week's gap between them. So I left it a couple of days, then wrote reporting it. I assumed that the card would have been cancelled…"

"I believe that it would have been cancelled today."

Neil calculated. How did the thief know the PIN number. Unless…

"Could you tell me your movements on Saturday, sir? Just to help us eliminate you from our enquiry."

"Certainly. I was working."

Willow had a cast-iron alibi for between eleven and three that afternoon. Alibis were odd things. People rarely had secure alibis for the majority of the time when they weren't at work. Too solid an alibi was itself suspicious. But it figured that if Willow taught the piano to private students, a lot of his work would be at the weekend.

"Thank you for your help, sir."

"Is that it?"

"That's it. I suggest you ring your bank to sort out a new card."

"That withdrawal put me into overdraft, you know. I'll have to pay charges."

"I'm sure that if you ring your bank, they'll help you sort something out."

"What did you think?" Neil asked Ben as they resumed their beat.

"Hmmm?"

Ben looked distracted. In fact, Neil realized, he'd been on edge all morning.

"He seemed fairly straight to me. What did you think?"

"Yeah. All right. I guess."

Neil stopped walking and glanced around. There was no one within listening distance.

"Something's on your mind, Ben. What is it?"

"Nothing particular."

"Come on," Neil insisted. "We're supposed to be mates. What is it? Has something gone on between you and Charly?"

"Hardly. She didn't come up this weekend."

Ben was never very comfortable talking about personal business.

"Had a row?" Neil asked, casually.

"Not really. She didn't call though. It isn't like her not to call."

He could have called her, Neil thought, but didn't say. Instead, he confided, "It can be a bit stressful, going out with a really good-looking woman. You're always worrying that there's someone else after her."

"It's not that," Ben told him. "The only thing between me and Charlene is work. She's trying to get a job here. That'd help a lot."

Neil spotted a rasta coming out of the pub who he needed to see about driving without documents. The two police officers walked over and the subject was dropped. The rasta made some excuses and promised to call in at the station later on with the relevant papers. Neil and Ben continued their beat. Most days on the beat were like this, Neil knew. He called them "nothing happening" days. They were the sort of days which seemed to last for ever. In a car, you always knew that something big could come up, even in the last ten minutes of a shift. You stayed on edge. But on the beat, it was different. Better, sometimes. You had more contact with people. But boring, too. He stamped his feet on the ground to defeat the cold. Only another five hours to go.

Paul Grace popped his head round the corner of the sergeant's office.

"Jan, I thought you'd like to know – you got on the course at the weekend."

"Good," Jan said. "Thank you."

Grace said "hello" to someone in the parade room then left. Jan cursed herself for being hypocritical. She didn't want to go on this course. Why was she thanking Grace, who had pushed her into it?

Baljit was in the parade room, writing up an arrest, his face dense with concentration. The Sikh officer looked very vulnerable, Jan thought, more like a preacher than a policeman.

"Where's John?" she asked, when Baljit looked up.

"Still in court. The case overran."

"Have you seen Carl?"

"He's out in a car on his own."

Jan nodded. She'd taken a look at Carl Price's personnel file last week. He liked to work on his own when possible. Nothing wrong with that, as long as he could play in a team, too. But there were a couple of complaints against him. One of them was from Clare Coppola, accusing Price of "persistent sexual harassment". The complaint hadn't been upheld, but Clare had been transferred and now Jan was her tutor. She didn't know who was in the right: Carl or Clare. The Italian girl could be really temperamental sometimes.

"Are you going to be long there?" she asked Baljit.

"Fifteen, twenty minutes."

"Would you go out with Carl when you're through?"

Baljit hesitated.

"I've got a few phone calls to make, Sarge."

"Can they wait?" Jan asked. "Thing is, it's one thing having an experienced officer out in a car on his own, but Carl is new to this beat. I know that you are too, but I'd prefer there to be two of you."

"Of course," Baljit said. "OK, Sarge."

"Thanks. I'll call him for you."

Carl Price didn't sound too pleased when Jan radioed him, but said he was heading back to the station. Jan took a car out on her own. She could have partnered Price herself, she supposed, but it seemed more appropriate to give him to a bloke.

Jan tried to think of the best way to tell Kevin that she had to go on a course this weekend.

Hopefully, his mother would have Henry, though she would complain about it. But Jan would get two days off in lieu. Maybe they could use them for a brief break in London. They'd been promising themselves a break as soon as Henry began to sleep through the night.

Jan was so preoccupied that she hardly noticed the incident until it was over. A youth was running away. A woman was getting up off the ground in front of a cashpoint machine. Jan turned her siren on, but she was heading the wrong way. By the time she'd turned round, the youth was gone. He'd run into the housing estate behind. She'd never catch him. Jan radioed a description in, then got out to join the woman who was dusting herself down.

"What happened?" Jan asked.

The woman pointed to the hole in the wall.

"I was getting some money out and, as I reached for it, he knocked me over, grabbed my purse, then took the money and ran. I tried to grab his leg, but…"

"Did you get a good look at him?"

"Not really. It all happened so fast."

"Did he speak at all?"

"Not a word."

Jan looked around. If there had been any other witnesses, they were long gone.

"Your card number," she said to the woman. "Do you think he saw it?"

"I don't know."

"Were you conscious of someone standing behind you?"

"There might have been. You know, I've had a long day. I'm tired. I really didn't notice."

"How much money did you take out?"

"Thirty pounds."

"And how much was there in your purse?"

"Not much. A few pounds. But it had my keys, and my credit card and…"

She was getting upset. Jan put a sympathetic hand on her shoulder.

"Don't worry. We'll sort it out. I'll drive you to the station. You can ring the bank about your cards from there…"

"Sarge?"

Carl and Baljit had arrived.

"White youth. Medium height and build, wearing a hooded kagoul and tracksuit bottoms. Ran off into the Maynard estate. Got a purse and thirty pounds. No witnesses apart from the victim. There's not much chance but you'd better have a look around."

"Any connection with the CID investigation?" Baljit asked, eagerly.

"I doubt it. But you never know."

The two young officers went off. Jan sighed. She'd been looking forward to having a quiet drive round, but it wasn't to be. That was the trouble with this job. Just when you were getting relaxed, you could count on it that someone would commit a crime.

It was late in the evening before Ben finally called Charlene. His pride felt that she ought to call him. Now he was expecting her answering machine and was surprised when she picked up the phone herself.

"Ben. I meant to call. I lost track of what shift you were on."

"Afternoons. How're things?"

"Hectic."

She launched into a long anecdote about what was going on at work. Ben feigned interest. Then he asked,

"Did you hear anything about that job in Nottingham?"

Charly hesitated.

"The interviews have been delayed," she said. "They rang me up and gave some garbled reason about other people on the shortlist being unavailable."

"So are you coming up this weekend?"

"Oh, sweetie, I can't. I'm up to my ears in…"

"Forget it."

"You could come here. We could have Saturday afternoon and evening."

Ben considered. This invitation was half-hearted

at best. If he went, he needed to be wanted. So he made up an excuse.

"Actually, I've got to do a football match on Saturday."

There was a pause which neither of them tried to interrupt. Then Charly spoke.

"Next weekend for sure."

"Can't. I'm working. Nights."

"Then I'll take some holiday and come and see you on your rest days."

"That'd be good."

He told her when his rest days were. Then he could hear her doorbell ringing in the background.

"I've got to go," she said. "Love you."

"You too."

They both hung up at the same time, the way they'd disciplined themselves to do when they first began living apart. Long distance love. It was difficult. Ben wasn't sure how much longer they could keep it up. And who was ringing Charly's doorbell at half past ten at night?

6

Most large police stations have CID attached to them. The detectives work closely with the uniforms, in theory at least. But this station didn't, and a visit from CID was a kind of honour. Usually, you were expected to go to them. Neil was very conscious of this, as Jan reintroduced him to Detective Inspector Ian Greasby.

"We're interested in this Willow character. I believe that you and a probationer interviewed him?"

"Yes, Ben here."

Greasby gave Ben a dismissive glance across the parade table and continued to address Neil.

"What impression did you get of Ray Willow?"

"Fairly standard victim. A bit nervous. Anxious about compensation."

"Honest?"

Neil considered.

"I wasn't sure. He didn't look me in the eye once. But then, if he was a villain, he probably would have done, wouldn't he? His body language was OK."

The sergeant nodded. Neil wondered if he was big on body language.

"I need to go through your notes, see if there are any contradictions."

"No problem."

"What's the latest?" he asked when the sergeant had finished. "Any leads?"

Greasby shrugged.

"You've got to understand that this is part of a national operation. We're collating phantom withdrawals which don't have a clear link with criminal activity. This might be one example, but I doubt it. We'll probably pick up a crooked postal worker somewhere along the line."

Greasby got out a card with his extension number on.

"You seem like a bright lad. See anything, hear anything to do with this, give me a call."

He scribbled his home number on the back, then winked as he handed it to Neil.

"This is the sort of investigation which makes careers. Bear it in mind."

"I will."

When he'd gone, Neil and Ben got ready to go

out on the beat. It was their last afternoon. Unless the sergeant was being a masochist, she would put them in a car when they were on nights, next week.

"You had any ideas on that Willow bloke?" Neil asked Ben.

Ben stopped studying the cloudy weather for a moment and thought about it.

"There was only one thing. He reported his card missing awfully quick. Let's say it was your card. You get the PIN number in the post ... how long would you wait before complaining that the card hadn't followed it?"

"A fortnight," Neil speculated. "More, if I was busy."

"Precisely. This guy wrote to them when it was two days late. Do you find that suspicious?"

"Just because he was paranoid..." Neil began.

"...doesn't mean that somebody wasn't out to get him. But maybe he protested too much, too soon."

"How could we prove that?"

"Find the man in the hat. Would you recognize him if you saw him again?"

Neil wasn't sure.

"Who knows? Maybe. All I got was a fleeting glimpse, side on."

"He's the one we need to find."

Neil agreed.

"But if Willow's involved with him, that blows CID's big conspiracy theory, doesn't it?"

"I'm not a big believer in conspiracy theories," Ben said. "Nine times out of ten, the simple explanation's the right one."

"And how do you recognize the other one in ten?" Neil asked.

Before Ben could answer, a call came in on the radio.

"Assault in progress. Youth and community centre. Bridge Street."

Neil spoke into his radio.

"4893 and 5117 responding. We're about five minutes away."

A fast walk to the centre took them four and a half minutes. Average response time was five, and they were feeling pleased with themselves until they saw that there was a car outside the centre. Carl Price and Baljit Singh were already in there.

"What's going on?" Neil asked.

Carl was dismissive.

"Kid got beaten up as he was coming away from the drinks machine. Nothing stolen. No big deal."

Baljit was leaning over an Asian youth. The boy was curled up on the floor of the centre entrance.

"Description?" Ben asked him.

Baljit shook his head.

"Two white lads got him from behind. Jeans, trainers, not much to go on."

"We'll ask around inside."

It was the middle of the afternoon. School was still on, so it was too early for there to be many people in the club. While Ben was interviewing a couple of lads by the pool table, Neil sought out the manager. All he found was a youth with a shaved head in the dingy back office.

"Are you the youth officer?"

"Nah. I'm the dogsbody. There's no one else on until four."

"Did you see what happened?"

"The lad who got knocked about? Nah."

"Was it you who called us?"

"Nah. Someone passing by, I think."

"Any idea what motivated the attack?"

"He rubbed somebody up the wrong way, I guess."

"Any idea who did it? Who was in here?"

The lad yawned.

"Didn't notice. I've only been working here a few days. I don't know all the faces yet."

"What about the victim?"

"Never seen him in here before."

Neil made a note of this.

"I thought you didn't know all the faces yet?"

"Yeah, but this one was a Paki, wasn't he? And this estate is nearly all white. He stood out."

"You're sure there's nothing else you can tell me?"

"Positive."

Neil left him. He met Ben in the corridor outside.

"Get an ID?"

Ben shook his head.

"No one saw, or heard, anything."

Outside, the victim was in the car. Beside it, Carl and Baljit were arguing about something.

"…waste of time."

"…just because you're a lazy, apathetic…"

It was down to him, Neil realized. Coppers weren't meant to undermine each other in public. Carl Price had been in the force longer than him, but Neil had more seniority on this shift.

"Problem?" he asked Price.

"Our friend here wants to put this in the racial incidents book."

"Why?"

"The victim says they called him a 'Paki bastard'," Baljit explained.

"Doesn't make it a racial incident," Carl insisted.

"They told him not to show his black face round here again."

"You put those words into his mouth," Price protested.

"I didn't. He…"

"Hey!"

Neil interrupted them.

"Take a statement at the station. The sarge'll decide if this goes in the racial incidents book. It's no big deal."

"It's more paperwork," Carl complained.

"I'm sure Baljit won't mind doing it."

"We were on our way to interview a suspect."

"So were we," Neil said. "I'm sure yours can wait."

Jan was about to knock off early so that she could get away for her course. Then Carl and Baljit walked into the station. An Asian youth with a bruised face stood between them.

"Word of advice, Sarge?" Carl asked.

Baljit was sitting the lad down, getting him a drink.

"Yes?"

"This lad got beaten up at a youth club. Old bed-spreadhead there wants to make it a racial incident."

"Either it is or it isn't," Jan snapped at Carl. "Why don't you ask him?"

Carl looked at Baljit, then raised his eyebrows.

"He's got a bee in his bonnet, Sarge. It's all a matter of interpretation, innit? We're meant to be keeping those figures down."

"No," Jan said. "We're meant to be keeping those figures *accurate*." The "Racial Incidents" log lay on a table with a lot of clutter which needed sorting out. Jan hadn't had cause to use it yet since starting her new job. While Carl went to get himself a drink, she walked over to the boy, who was sat on his own.

"Any idea why they jumped you?" Jan asked.

"No. I just went in to use the drinks machine," the boy replied, sullenly. "They said I wasn't allowed. I said why not? They started beating me up, calling me 'Paki bastard, Paki bastard'. They left me on the steps." Fifty-fifty, Jan decided. The question was, who did she want to humour: Carl or Baljit?

"Can I have a word, Sarge?"

Baljit was putting down the drink for the boy.

"If it's quick," Jan told him.

In her office, Baljit spoke nervously.

"I was meant to be partnered with PC Farraday, but I seem to be stuck with PC Price instead."

"It's a day to day thing," Jan told him. "John and Tim have had a couple of court cases."

"Neither of them have got one today."

He was right, she realized. John and Tim liked to work together and she had let the matter slide.

"I'm sorry, Baljit. I'll get it changed next…"

She checked her diary.

"I see they're both in court on Tuesday, so they'll miss the first night. Maybe…"

"Perhaps I could work on my own for a few days then, on foot patrol."

"At night?"

No one wanted to go out walking at night.

"There's something I want to look into."

"I'll think about it," Jan promised, half-heartedly.

"Thank you. And about the attack? Is it a racial incident?"

Jan stood up and checked her watch. She was late.

"It's your call," she told Baljit. "Do what you think is the right thing."

"The bank still haven't settled with me."

"It's only been a few days, Mr Willow."

"And why are you harassing me? Am I supposed to have done something?"

Neil put on his most patient, beleaguered expression.

"We only wanted to see if you'd remembered anything else ... unusual ... which might be of use to us in the investigation, sir."

"Like what ... a flying green alien which invades my house and snatches bank cards from the mail before I've had time to look at it?"

Ben laughed politely. You came across all sorts of humour in this job and it was best to act as if you saw the joke, no matter how sick or silly.

"It occurred to us, Mr Willow, that you reported the card missing very quickly, within – what was it – two or three days of when it should have come. We thought that you perhaps had a reason for thinking that it had gone astray."

The music teacher was impatient.

"It's a good thing I did, isn't it? If the card had

been used before I'd reported it, I'd have been liable, wouldn't I?"

This wasn't true, but neither Ben nor Neil told him this. It was a useful indicator of his state of mind. Ben repeated the question.

"Was there anything which made you suspicious, Mr Willow?"

"I'm suspicious of everybody, of everything. Aren't you two?"

Ben smiled and got up to go.

"Not everything, sir. But perhaps we ought to be."

"Made up your mind?" Neil asked, as they walked back towards the station.

"If he was involved?" Ben considered. "Not really. People like that, on edge all the time, they're the hardest to read, aren't they?"

Neil accepted this.

"Off to London this weekend?"

Ben shook his head.

"Charly's too busy. Exams coming up. I'm putting in overtime at the match."

"Rather you than me."

Neil used to do all the overtime he could manage but, since getting back together with Clare, preferred to hold on to his time off. And if County were playing, he liked to be on the terraces, not on duty.

"Charly's coming over on my next rest days though," Ben told him.

"That's good," Neil said.

He meant it. A couple of days of tender, loving care from his girlfriend was what Ben needed, Neil reckoned. Ben seemed uptight most of the time these days. It wasn't good for him.

School was out as they walked past the youth centre. There were a bunch of boys walking in. A couple of them greeted the worker who Neil had interviewed earlier, Jed something. The lad was standing by the noticeboard. Ben stopped and stared at the entrance until they'd all gone inside.

"Something wrong?" Neil asked him. "Want to go in and have another look?"

"Not now," Ben told him. "When they're not expecting it."

Expecting what? Neil wondered. But then an old lady came up to them to complain about the noise from her upstairs neighbour's television set and Neil forgot to ask.

7

Jan Hunt was uncomfortable. She'd never liked being a student much, listening to lectures. But this lecture felt more like a telling off.

"More custodial sentences. Higher fines. A bigger chance of being found guilty. Why do these things happen to black people? What does the system say?" The speaker paused for effect. "The system says that black people get discriminated against because *they deserve it*. We should never have been allowed in this country in the first place. We should never have been allowed to breed. And if we don't like the way we're treated then we should go back to where we came from. Am I right?"

There was an embarrassed silence. You didn't argue with statistics like the ones they had been given. Although statistics could be made to say anything, Jan knew.

"You officers are here voluntarily. I applaud that. Although doubtless this course will look good on your *curriculum vitaes*. Originally, there was a plan for every officer in the country to come on a course like this. Then it was costed. They decided it would be a lot cheaper to issue a leaflet instead."

He held up the leaflet on racial and sexual harassment. Jan didn't remember seeing one before. It must have come out while she was on maternity leave.

"We all have prejudices. Prejudice comes from ignorance and fear. Many of you are ignorant about black people in Britain today. Put your hand up if you have one close friend who is black."

No one put their hand up. The speaker didn't look surprised.

"Ignorance creates prejudice. But prejudice alone does not make you a racist. Acting on those prejudices does. Prejudice plus power plus action equals racism. In your job, you have a lot of power and, therefore, a great responsibility to use it properly. The aim of this course is not to make you feel guilty. Guilt is negative. The aim of this course is to make you aware."

Jan was aware that she would much rather be at home, in bed, with her husband, enjoying one of those rare weekends when they were both off work.

* * *

Ruth hadn't been to the bookshop since the raid a fortnight before. Because of the attack, she hadn't had a chance to look around it properly, so today seemed like a good opportunity. All of the damage had been repaired. The shop looked much like it had before, only sparser, tidier. One of the workers, recognizing Ruth, said hello. Ruth smiled back. It was nice to be recognized in a new city. It helped her to feel like she belonged.

Ruth picked up a novel by Margaret Atwood to read over the weekend. She would save money if she got up early enough to go into the city before the library closed, but her lie-ins were precious. Next, she went over to the accommodation board. There was less than a month before this module ended and Ruth was fed up of living alone. She was worried that if Neil got a house before she and Clare found somewhere to live, then Clare would move in with him, instead. Ruth wouldn't blame her. She'd had enough of living with her parents long ago.

There was one card which looked vaguely promising.

HOUSE SHARE IN FOREST FIELDS
2 people wanted ASAP
— students or DSS welcome —
·own room· share bills·
·TV· video· microwave·
(no smokers or pets please!)
ring 555723

There was a date when the card had gone up, only the week before. Ruth copied down the details, then paid for the book. A notice on the counter explained what had happened two Saturdays before and said that the bookshop collective would be sponsoring a demonstration after the attackers had been to court, next month. Ruth signed her name and address to a list of people wanting information about the demo. Leaving the shop, she realized that she might not be able to go on it. Police officers weren't allowed to get involved in political groups. Was an anti-racist march classed as political? She didn't know.

Ruth walked over to the Victoria Centre. She was meeting a couple of people from her shift for a drink that evening. She was fed up of wearing the same clothes every time she went out. A new top, at least, would be nice. She browsed for nearly an hour, until she found a bright, cotton one which she liked, in River Island. But when she went to pay for it, she found that she didn't have her cheque book on her or enough cash to buy it. It was embarrassing.

Ruth did some mental arithmetic. If she took out another twenty pounds she'd have enough left in her account to pay the standing order for her rent and keep her going until the end of the month, just. There was a cashpoint machine inside the Victoria Centre which took her "Link" card. She left the top with the assistant at the till. Then she walked through the crowded shopping centre to the machine.

There was a queue and she joined it. Ruth didn't mind queueing. She really enjoyed shopping. It was relaxing. She thought about the blouse she was buying and how it looked on her. Clothes were better value for money than books, she decided. A book you read once, twice at most. A good top lasted for years.

Finally she got to the front of the queue, withdrew twenty pounds and turned to walk away. It was then that she recognized him. He was wearing a woolly hat, so that you couldn't see his shaved head, or the boot tattooed across his forehead. But Ruth was sure that he was the one she'd seen a fortnight before, the one who'd shouted at her. He was also the one who'd knocked the disabled woman out of her wheelchair. He hadn't been in the police cell that evening, or she'd have recognized him, she was sure. She wouldn't have forgotten him until now. He must have been one of the ones who got away.

The centre was crowded with Saturday afternoon shoppers. It was easy for Ruth to mingle with them, following the guy from a distance. Only when he was half a mile away from the centre, heading for the outskirts of the city, did Ruth remember the top, waiting to be paid for in a bag beneath the counter. She would have to wear her denim shirt tonight instead.

None of the attackers were from Nottingham, Ruth knew. Half of them had been arrested trying to get home on the Heanor bus. Most of the others were from Mansfield. So what was this guy doing in the city? Ruth watched as the skinhead turned into a building. Then she got close enough to read the sign on the front of it: Youth and Community Centre.

Ruth stood outside the centre, pretending that she was waiting for the phone box. A few people went in, a couple of them skinheads, like the one she'd followed, only younger. Nobody left. The shops were about to close, she realized. Maybe it was time to go. She was on the wrong side of town to walk home. She had to go back to Friar Lane to catch a bus, pick up something for her dinner on the way.

Another short-haired youth arrived. He gave Ruth a long, hard stare before going inside. Ruth realized that there was no longer anybody in the phone box. She rang central station, and gave the information about the skinhead she had seen to someone on the switchboard.

"Do you want me to stay here?" she asked, after she'd finished explaining.

"I'm not sure whether we'll be able to get anyone there. We're short-staffed and the football people have just gone off duty. But I'll make sure CID get the information on Monday morning."

Great, thought Ruth, just great. But then, what were the chances of a successful arrest? Hadn't she told the investigating officers that she couldn't identify any of the attackers apart from the young one? Only when she'd seen him again did she recognize his face, remember the tattoo. It wouldn't hold up in court.

Should she go into the centre? No. It was too risky. She didn't even have her warrant card on her. She'd give Clare a ring before she went out, talk it over with her. Ruth checked her watch again, wondered if River Island stayed open until six. Then, without looking round, she hurried back towards town.

The match finished in a one-one draw. This was always the best result for the police because it gave neither set of supporters cause to get too aggrieved afterwards. There was no trouble. Ben helped escort the rival fans to the railway station, then he was through. He got changed and started to head into town, unsure what to do for the rest of the day. In the subway which led to the Broadmarsh shopping centre, a busker was singing "keep on rocking in the free world". Ben smiled, thinking of the overtime he'd just earned, and gave the man twenty pence.

He was free tonight, or as free as he wanted to be. So why did he feel like returning to the railway station, joining Charlene for the evening? It wasn't too late. Ben stopped by the phone booths in front of HMV and pulled out his phone card. He hadn't got his luggage with him, but so what? He had a set of toiletries at Charly's and he was thirty seconds away from Marks and Spencer's. He could buy himself some spare underwear. The phone rang four times.

"Hi, this is Charlene. I'm afraid that I can't take your call right now, but if you'd like to leave a message..."

Ben cursed and hung up. What had stopped him going when they spoke the other night? Why had he insisted on doing the match instead? It was something to do with foolish pride. She didn't want him enough. He had only himself to blame if his foolish pride led his girlfriend into another man's arms.

Work was the only thing which took his mind off his relationship with Charly. Ben strode across town quickly, remembering something he'd seen yesterday afternoon. The boy in the youth centre had been the same one who'd attacked Jatinder's shop. Ben was almost sure of it. All right, Jatinder wouldn't press charges, but Ben could still hassle the lad, put the fear of God in him. He wanted to know his name, find out what he was up to. Why not do it now?

At least the morning session had been lively. Now Jan was stuck in another lecture and having trouble keeping awake. At Poly, she used to take notes all the time in order to stop her from dozing off. This afternoon, she couldn't be bothered. A middle-aged academic type was going on about the rise of the new right in Europe.

"As the recession deepens, neo-fascist parties have won election after election, in Italy, in Germany, even in France, a short tunnel journey away. You might say that it can never happen here, but you shouldn't be so sure. The National Front were seen off in the nineteen-seventies. Groups like the old Anti-Nazi league and Rock Against Racism deserve some of the credit for that, but not the majority. The main reason for the decline of racist parties in the seventies was that Margaret Thatcher adopted much of their agenda and won their voters. Do you remember her speech about not wanting to be 'swamped' by people from other cultures?"

Jan failed to suppress a yawn.

"The main racist organization active today is the British National Party, founded from the embers of the old National Front in 1982. And there are other smaller, more violent, even paramilitary groups which are more recent. They're active in London, and particularly in parts of the East Midlands. They've started in medium-sized towns like Ilkeston and Mansfield, but they'll be moving into the big cities with large immigrant populations as soon as they're strong enough: Leicester, quite possibly, or Nottingham..."

Jan clicked awake. The guy was exaggerating, she

thought. There were incidents, attacks where race was a contributory factor, but heavily organized racist violence? She didn't believe it.

"How do you recognize these groups? A lot of them retain a deep admiration for Adolf Hitler, so swastikas are a dead giveaway. The slogan 'Tomorrow is ours' is a less obvious sign, also taken from the Nazis. Other racists call themselves 'Odinists'. They believe in ethnic purity, based on a semi-mythical Norse ancestry. Then there are…"

Jan had stopped listening again. She was thinking about the attack on the lad outside the youth centre on Friday. She'd got it wrong, she decided: if race was a contributory factor then it *was* a racial incident, every time. Later on, she'd check precisely what the official definition was.

The group met in the back room of the youth centre. Jed had helped to pick likely candidates. You couldn't hurry a job like this – he'd only been working there a week, after all – but there were half a dozen of them, not counting Brig, who'd come over from Hucknall to give the recruiting talk.

"What's unemployment on this estate?" Brig asked. "Fifty per cent? More? Why do you think that is?"

"Government," one of the brighter youths dared.

"Nah. Them in parliament, they're all the same.

They're all nigger lovers. Some of them are niggers themselves. The reason there's so many unemployed is that there aren't enough jobs to go round. Why aren't there enough jobs to go round?"

"Because the blacks have got them," suggested Chas, who was currently suspended from school after being caught beating up twelve-year-olds for their dinner money.

"Precisely," Brig told him.

Chas looked proud. Jed knew the routine. Once Brig had convinced them that all you had to do was to send all the blacks home, he'd move on to the Jews and why Hitler should never have been our enemy. Some people took exception to glorifying old Adolf. As a rule, people didn't join because they were into Nazi paraphernalia. That came later. They joined because they wanted to break some heads, to smash things up, like they'd done in the bookshop. Jed asked Brig when the next action was.

"The lefties are bound to have some sort of demo, to protest about the bookshop raid."

"When?"

"Dunno. It'll probably take them a month to get it together."

"And we're going to break it up?" Jed asked, enthusiastically.

"Mebbe. But I don't know if you'll be allowed along. You might get into too much bother if you get done again before their court date."

"But I'm not going to court," Jed told him. "I only got a caution."

"I'd forgotten that," Brig said.

"So we can come along?" one of the new recruits asked. "How will we know where to come?"

"We'll let you know. But Jed, you might be better off behind the scenes for a while. Know what I mean?"

Jed nodded. If he got into trouble, he might lose this job. And, as Brig had pointed out, this was a good recruiting ground. Jed wondered what Mr Jagger would think if he knew what he was getting up to. The solicitor thought that he was doing Jed a favour by getting him this job. Jed wondered if he knew what kind of a favour it was.

Ben noticed someone he thought he recognized walking away as he was arriving, but he couldn't be sure. Then he walked into the youth centre and inspected the noticeboard. He found what he was looking for and tore it off. It took him five minutes to find the manager, a long-haired man in his thirties, with a shapeless sweater and dirty jeans.

"You've got a lad working here, about five-ten, very short hair, wiry. Know who I mean?"

The man nodded.

"Jed, his name is. On the Youth Training Scheme. Only been with us a couple of weeks."

"Can I speak to him?"

"Sorry. He doesn't work weekends unless there's some kind of do on. You're not a regular here, are you? What do you want?"

Ben flashed his warrant card.

"Who's responsible for the noticeboard in the entrance hall?"

"Jed, mainly. Why do you ask?"

"Did he put this up?"

Ben held up the recruiting leaflet he'd spotted earlier. The manager examined it.

"Dunno. We get all types in here, some of them have funny ideas. But if I'd noticed this, I'd have torn it down, I can assure you."

"Mind if I have a look around?"

"Be my guest."

Ben wasn't in uniform any more, so the guy probably thought he was CID. Having got this far, he ought to go, return on Monday. Yet something smelt wrong. The manager was behind him, not exactly following, but hanging around.

"Is this about that bit of trouble yesterday?" he asked. "I wasn't on duty when…"

"I know," Ben said, trying the door of a side room, which turned out to be locked. "What's in here?"

The manager hesitated. Ben thought that he'd heard voices, but they stopped when he tried the handle.

"Private meeting," said the manager.

"Whose private meeting?"

"The lad you were talking about. Jed."

"I thought you told me that he wasn't here today?"

"I said that he wasn't working."

"I hope that this meeting appears in your booking sheet."

The manager didn't reply. Ben turned the door handle.

"Hold on," the manager said. "I won't be responsible for what'll happen if…"

The door opened.

"Who…?"

Ben barged into the dark room. He recognized Jed – the youth from the shop attack in Mansfield – who was standing at the door. There were seven people sat around the table. Five of them were youths. Two were older. The biggest had a boot tattooed across his forehead. He was the one who spoke.

"Shut the door."

"But…"

The manager tried to splutter some words out but one of them slammed the door in his face. The tattooed skinhead stood.

"Say your prayers, you black bastard. You've just entered your worst nightmare."

8

A racially motivated incident is:

a) any incident in which it appears to the reporting or investigating officer that the complaint involves an element of racial motivation, or

b) any incident which includes an allegation of racial motivation by any persons.

"Incidents" include verbal abuse, threatening behaviour, graffiti, damage to property, physical attack, arson, and murder.

ASSOCIATION OF POLICE OFFICERS 1989

Jan put the piece of paper down.

"Does that help you, Sergeant?" the instructor asked.

"Yes. Thank you."

"Good. Now, what we're looking at in this session is how racial discrimination can take place in the police force itself. We'll be looking at some real case studies taken from successful complaints against the Notts police force…"

This was more interesting, Jan decided.

"I'm going to start by showing you something you probably didn't have time to watch when it was first broadcast."

The figure *4* appeared on the screen. Jan groaned. Had she come all this way to watch a Channel 4 documentary? Yet, as the story in the *Dispatches* programme began to unfold, she found herself watching with a combination of fascination and unease.

The programme was about three Asian police officers, each of whom had been given a three month attachment to Notts CID back in the 1980s. Of twenty-three people attached to CID during that period, only three had failed to get permanent CID postings – the three Asians.

Actors playing senior officers stonewalled as the case against the force got stronger and stronger. One black CID officer described how he had ignored racist banter at first and was treated as one of the lads. Eventually, though, his pride couldn't take it any more. As soon as he complained, he was frozen out. But banter was the least of it. Black officers were given much less support than white ones. When they complained, allegations were made up or exaggerated to justify not offering them CID jobs.

The whole thing made Jan sick. And it wasn't only because what was happening was wrong. She was sick because she recognized the situations. She found herself thinking about Baljit Singh. How would he feel, watching this? Would he recognize Jan's behaviour, failing to fix him up with an experienced partner? She found herself thinking about Ben Shipman.

"That's enough," Jed said. "Go on, you'd better get out of here. Someone might of called the police."

Reluctantly, all seven of them stopped kicking the black guy. Brig slapped Jed on the back on his way out. When they'd gone, Jed looked at the black guy, who was now wheezing on the floor. He had received a professional kicking. They'd left his face, apart from a cut beneath the eye and a swollen ear. But his body, beneath the jeans and blouson, would be covered with bruises.

The guy opened his eyes and stared at Jed. Jed stared right back.

"What do you want me to do?" he asked. "Call an ambulance? Call the police?"

"Why would you do that?" the bruised geezer asked. His voice, though croaky, was obviously educated.

"Look, you soft idiot," Jed said. "You can claim that you were beaten up in here, but I'll say that we found you outside, that we brought you in here before the police arrived. You got knocked about the head, so you were confused. Now, who're they going to believe? Me, who'll find witnesses to back me up, or some silly sod stupid enough to walk straight into a Nazi meeting?"

"I didn't know what it was," the man mumbled.

"Well, then," Jed told him, "I guess you should have knocked."

The bloke was getting his breath back a bit. He sat up.

"Why do you do this?" he asked. "What did I ever do to you?"

Jed thought for a moment.

"Personally," he said, "I haven't got anything against Africans, or wherever it is that you're from. It's Pakis I don't like, Pakis and Indians. You lot, you're not much different from us, but they're filth. Know what I mean?"

"Not really."

"Trouble is ... my friends who just left, they don't make such fine distinctions. They reckon…"

He was interrupted by the door opening. It was Laurie, the stupid wimp who managed the place.

"What do you want?"

"I tried to warn you," Laurie said, "but you slammed the door in my face."

"Tried to warn me what?"

Laurie didn't answer. Instead he turned to the black bloke, who was slowly standing up.

"Are you all right?" Laurie asked.

"I'll live."

"Want me to call an ambulance? The police station?"

The guy shook his head. He knew what was good for him.

"Just get me a taxi."

Jed tried to ask Laurie what he'd meant about warning him, but the black guy waved an arm at the centre manager.

"Leave us."

And Laurie did. Jed couldn't believe it – Laurie taking orders from a black guy ten years younger than him.

"I've seen you before," the black bloke said, "in Mansfield." Jed recognized him now. He'd been in the shop they did over the week before.

"I remember," he told the bloke now. "You did right both times, not calling the police."

"Not much point," the guy replied, pulling something from his back pocket. "You see, I *am* the police."

9

It was late on Saturday afternoon. The estate agent, unusually, had given Neil a key to the empty house, told him to drop it back in on Monday. When they got there, he understood why they'd trusted him. The place was practically empty. Thieves had been in and ripped out the fireplace. All that was left were the carpets on the floor and a couple of pieces of furniture too large to remove easily. They went upstairs. The bedrooms were a good size, but equally delapidated. Neil could see why the place was so cheap.

"It's got character," Clare said.

"You mean you like it?"

She didn't reply. They looked in the bathroom. There was no bath, only a shower cubicle. Neil opened the door. There was something growing in it.

"Let's go back downstairs," Clare suggested.

He followed her down. She stood in the living-room, staring at the overgrown garden. Maybe she really does like it, he thought. If she likes the place enough, I'll buy it, even though it feels like a mausoleum.

"Shall we go?" he suggested mildly.

"I was just thinking…" Clare said.

Here we go, Neil thought.

"We hardly get any time in a house together, alone." Clare was always capable of taking Neil by surprise. She went on. "It'll be weeks before I find a place, and, even then, Ruth'll be there a lot of the time. And buying a house takes *months*…"

"What are you saying?" Neil asked.

"All I'm saying it that we don't have to rush away from this dump."

Neil laughed softly.

"I guess not."

"The sofa looks pretty clean."

They sat down together. Clare took off her duffle-coat.

"Oooh, it's cold in here. You'll have to warm me up."

Neil took off his coat too. Then he snuggled up next to her and began to kiss her pale, white neck.

"That won't be a problem."

He was beginning to like this house, after all.

"I'm sorry, Ruth. Clare's out with Neil. I don't know when to expect her back."

"OK. Thanks."

Ruth put down the phone, then had another idea and rang directory enquiries. She got the number she wanted and called it. The phone kept ringing. Odd, she thought. He seemed like the sort of person who would have an answering machine. She was about to put the phone down when he picked up.

"Ben?"

"Yeah."

"It's Ruth Clarke here. Look, I'm sorry, I didn't wake you up or something, did I?"

"Not exactly."

"You sound funny."

"It's a long story. I need to get into a bath."

Oh God, Ruth thought. Suppose I've interrupted him with his girlfriend?

"The thing is, I saw something this afternoon which I thought might interest you and Neil. Now I know it's your day off, so tell me to get lost if you like but…"

"Were you at the youth and community centre?"

"Yes. How did you…?"

"I was there too."

He paused. Ruth wasn't sure whether to tell him what she knew, or wait.

"Look," Ben said, "I need to talk this over with someone, but I can't speak now. What are you doing later?"

Ruth hesitated.

"I'm meeting some friends for a drink, but I don't mind…"

"Where?"

"The Peacock, about half eight."

"Would it be all right if I joined you?"

"Sure."

Ruth wished she hadn't mentioned the friends. She'd rather see him some place where it was just the two of them. But he's got a girlfriend, she reminded herself. This meeting was going to be professional.

"If I don't show up —" Ben was blowing her out in advance — "it's because I'm not well."

"What's wrong?"

"I'll tell you later. Give me your number, would you? If I don't make it, I'll call you tomorrow."

So now he has my number, Ruth thought, putting the phone down. That's a start. But he sounded like he was ill. She wondered what was wrong with him.

When Ben got out of the bath he felt worse than when he'd got in. Slowly, painfully, he got dressed. Why had he agreed to meet Ruth tonight? Because he didn't want to be alone. He examined himself in the mirror, then put a plaster on his left ear. One of his eyes was all puffed up, so he put on a pair of sunglasses. They made him look like a drug dealer, or a pimp. Charly hated them. But he wasn't going out with Charly tonight. If she'd been in when he called her earlier, none of this need have happened.

Normally, it took him fifteen minutes to walk briskly to where the pub was. This evening, though, it took him more than five minutes to limp to the main road for a bus. He hoped that he'd be well enough to work tomorrow. It would look bad if he didn't.

Luckily, the bus stopped directly opposite the pub. Ben felt a little faint as he pressed the button on the pedestrian crossing. The Peacock, when he got to it, was crowded. He couldn't see Ruth Clarke in either bar. He couldn't make out anybody at the tables for the crowd around the bar. Nor did he have the energy to push his way through. Coming out had been stupid, he decided. He would ring Ruth tomorrow.

As he was leaving the pub, someone was coming out of the opposite bar room. He had glanced in the snug on his way in and Ruth hadn't been there. Yet now he saw her, sitting down at a table by the door. She must have been in the loo before. Seeing him, she smiled and waved.

"Ben. You made it."

He smiled weakly.

"You look dreadful. Why are you wearing sun-glasses in February?"

Before he could answer, she carried on talking.

"Never mind. What are you drinking? Then I'll introduce you to everyone."

Ben could tell at a glance that Ruth's companions were all police officers. They must be from the relief that she was attached to. A couple of them nodded amiably at Ben but didn't try to make space for him to sit down. Luckily, as he glanced around, a couple at the other end of the room were leaving. If he was quick, he could get one of their stools. But it wasn't easy for him to be quick at the moment. As he pushed his way towards the vacant stools, he heard one of Ruth's companions asking who he was.

"Some spook stud she picked up in a club."

"No," one of the others said in a lower voice. "I recognize him. He's in the job."

"Are you OK?"

Ruth was behind him, holding his pint of shandy.

"I'm not sure I'm up to the company."

"You don't look up to much," she told him, in a kind voice. "Why don't you sit down here? I'll get my drink and join you. This lot are beginning to bore me anyway."

Gratefully, he collapsed into a corner.

When she got back, he asked her what she was doing outside the youth centre earlier on. She told him about following a bloke who had been involved in the attack on the bookshop two weeks before. From her description, Ben recognized the brute who'd led the beating which he'd received that afternoon. When she'd finished, he told her about it.

"You poor lamb!" Ruth said. "Why didn't you call the police?"

Ben shrugged.

"I was a bit embarrassed," he told her. "I thought I'd made a fool of myself, going in there. And they'd never have caught them – only the lad, Jed. And all he did was organize the meeting. He didn't attack me himself."

"I thought you said he was involved in an attack on your friend's shop?"

"Yes. But Jatinder won't press charges. The lad'll probably get the sack for organizing a racist meeting. That's punishment enough."

"So that's it then?" Ruth asked. "You've driven them out of one place and you're satisfied with that? You don't think that they'll just start up again somewhere else on the same estate?"

"I'm not responsible for smashing the racist movement single handed!" Ben protested.

"Yes you are," Ruth told him. "We all are."

"You sound just like my girlfriend," Ben told her. Ruth winced.

"Anyway," she said, changing the subject. "What did they say at hospital? No broken bones?"

"I haven't been to hospital."

Ruth looked shocked.

"*Haven't been?* You're walking like a cripple. You could have broken ribs, or a fractured skull."

"I'm all right."

"Like hell you are. Come on."

She stood up.

"I'm driving you to Casualty."

"I don't think…"

Ruth spoke sternly.

"You need looking after, you do. If your girlfriend was here, instead of in London, she wouldn't have let you out tonight. She'd have taken you there. But she isn't. So I'm going to do it instead. All right?"

Ben was too tired to argue. It was a relief to let someone look after him. She was just being friendly, he thought, as she took his arm and helped him towards her car. There was nothing physical going on. But he was too tired to think about that, either.

10

The night shift began with another mugging and cash card theft from the machine on the Maynard Estate. Jan let Baljit pick the call up on his own, which surprised Neil.

"Course good, Sarge?" Neil asked, when the Asian officer had gone.

"I'll tell you about it later. I've got bad news, I'm afraid. Ben's off sick. I want you to partner Carl."

"I thought he was with Baljit?"

"No. Baljit's on his own for a couple of days, then he's back with John. Now, I want the two of you to look in on the youth and community centre before it closes. I'll tell you why."

When she'd finished talking, Neil felt his blood boil.

"He was a stupid prat, wasn't he?" Carl Price said, as they walked towards the youth centre. "Going in on his own like that."

"He had no way of knowing that there was a bunch of racist thugs holding a recruiting session in there."

Price laughed.

"What's so funny?"

"I was imagining the look on Shipman's face when he walked into that room."

"That's my partner you're talking about," Neil snapped.

Price had the grace to look embarrassed.

"Yeah, sorry. Everyone says he's a good copper."

More than everyone says about you, Neil thought.

The manager of the youth centre, Laurie Jones, was apologetic.

"I had no idea what was going on."

"Is Jed Sutcliffe in tonight?" Neil asked.

"No. I suspended him."

"How long for?"

"Until the committee meets. Then I expect he'll get the sack. Openly supporting racist organizations is a sacking offence in any city council job."

"Who's on the management committee?" Neil wanted to know.

The manager gave them a list: a lawyer, two councillors, a JP, someone from the tenants' association. None of the names meant anything to Neil.

"Which of these appointed Sutcliffe?"

"Mr Jagger. He's the chairman."

This sounded curious to Neil.

"Him on his own?"

"Yes, well, I had a word with Jed too, of course."

"I'm curious as to why someone would come all the way from Mansfield for a badly paid job like this one."

"Maybe it was the only job he could get."

Carl Price shuffled his feet and gave Neil a look. He didn't know where these questions were leading. Neither did Neil, but sometimes you had to fish around in order to find something you didn't know was there. According to Jan, who'd spoken to Ben on the phone, the manager had known enough about who was in the meeting to try and warn Ben off. But now he was pleading ignorance. There was something dodgy going on – something which hadn't come out yet. Neil wanted to know what it was.

"When do we question this Sutcliffe kid?" Carl asked, as they walked away from the centre.

"We're leaving him to stew for a while. Ben thinks it's unlikely we'll get anything out of him about the other attackers. We need to keep our eyes open, see if anyone drops a name we can confront Sutcliffe with."

A police car drove past them. Baljit Singh waved. Neil gave him a thumbs up sign. Carl ignored him.

"Something wrong between you two?"

"He's off on some wild goose chase," Carl complained. "Talk about methodical – he does everything by the numbers and at half speed."

"Nothing wrong with being thorough."

"*Thorough?* He can't see the wood for the trees, that's his problem. Nearly didn't pass probation and he's scared of getting the push. If he wasn't a wog, he wouldn't have a job by now. He's useless. But they've got so few Pakis on the force they like to keep them around, don't they? Public relations."

"I don't like that kind of talk," Neil said, firmly.

"What?" Price seemed surprised by Neil's reaction.

"Wogs, Pakis. You're out of order."

"Oh, come on," Price said. "There's no one listening to us. You know that whites are better at the job than blacks. Only you won't say it out loud 'cause you think it'll hurt your chances. I can play that game too. But don't give me any of that *we're all equal* crap – you don't believe it any more than I do."

"You're right," Neil said, sarcastically. "We're not all equal. Some people are better than others. But colour's got nothing to do with it. Use words like that around me again and I'll report you. All right?"

The two men faced off for a moment. Price broke the stare.

"Yes," he said, in an irritated voice. "All right."

They walked in uncomfortable silence for five minutes. Neil didn't like walking at night, but it was important to have people around at this time, as the pubs were closing.

"Let's have a look in the Rose and Crown, shall we?" Neil said, to break the tension. It was eleven minutes past eleven. According to the letter of the law, everyone should have finished drinking up by now, but they wouldn't have. The moment Neil and Carl appeared on the threshold of the public bar, they heard the landlord begin shouting:

"Come on now, ladies and gentlemen, let's be having your glasses please. It's gone time. Drink up or leave it behind."

The two officers had a quick look round to let themselves be seen. This was a genteel pub. There was rarely any trouble, so the police usually left it alone. Neil went into the lounge bar to get Carl Price, who was chatting up a barmaid.

"Going?" Price asked.

"Yes," Neil replied, then saw something. "Hold on."

"What is it?"

"Don't turn around."

Neil spoke to the barmaid in a low, urgent voice.

"That bloke in the green sweater, do you know him?"

"You mean the one talking to the music teacher?"

"That's the one."

"Ted something ... he's in here two or three nights a week."

"Is he often with Ray Wi ... the music teacher?"

"Not as far as I know. They're not big mates or anything like that."

"Do you know what this Ted does or where he lives?"

"He lives nearby, I think. I guess he's on the dole. I often see him around during the day."

"Thanks. We didn't have this conversation, all right?"

The girl smiled at him.

"Since it's you asking, go on. I'd rather talk to you than your friend there."

He's not my friend, Neil felt like saying, but buttoned it. He walked out of the bar, keeping his back to the drinkers, hoping that Willow wouldn't recognize him. Carl followed.

"What are we doing?"

"Splitting up," Neil said. "The bloke I was talking about – the green sweater – I want you to follow him, find out where he lives, then radio me. OK?"

"If you say so. Why?"

Neil filled him in as quickly as possible, then radioed the station to let them know what was going on. He felt his adrenaline surging. He'd rather be getting the blokes who beat up Ben, but this would be a good second best. He followed Ray Willow home from a distance. Then he waited outside the house until Carl radioed him. It didn't take long. Next, Neil rang Jan at the station, got her to check the electoral register for him. Within two minutes, he had a name.

"I'd like permission to go in and question him, Sarge," Neil said.

"I'm not sure," she said. "CID will be annoyed if we don't leave it for them until the morning."

"We've got them both in their homes now. If I go in straight away, there's no chance of them making contact with each other. We can nail them."

"I'll tell you what," Jan said. "I'll call Inspector Grace. Hold your horses."

Neil stood in the shadows of a tree, watching Willow's house. The downstairs light went off. Then the upstairs landing light went off. Another light, presumably the bathroom, was switched on. Then Jan's voice came on the radio.

"Inspector Grace says that you can question him, provided he's not drunk."

"He looked sober enough walking home," Neil told her. "What about his partner?"

"If he is the partner," Jan said, "then I'll take him with Carl. I'll go over there in a car now. Good luck."

"Thanks, Sarge."

The bathroom light went off and the bedroom light came on. No sweet dreams for you tonight, Neil thought, as he rang the doorbell.

11

Getting the pig's blood had been the hardest thing. It wasn't that easy these days, finding a friendly butcher who wouldn't ask awkward questions. Jed used one in Mansfield, a party supporter. After what happened on Saturday, Jed needed to prove himself again. His partner tonight was Kirk. Kirk was a bit of a legend in far right circles. He was in his mid-thirties now. His short hair had a couple of grey patches and his acne-pocked skin was old and sallow looking. But this was the man who was reputed to have single-handedly set up a race riot in Rotherham. As they drove along the Woodborough Road, waiting for it to be quiet enough to strike, Jed asked him all about it.

"The thing about the left," Kirk boasted, "is that

they're paranoid. They turn one bloke with a thousand stickers into a huge far right presence."

"What about the police?" Jed asked. "Did they get in your way?"

"In our way? Hah. Half of them support us, never forget that. When the riot happened, who got arrested? The lefties, that's who. All our lot escaped."

Jed was about to ask how Kirk had orchestrated the "riot", where a bunch of racists smashed up an Anti-Nazi League demonstration. It would be useful to know for when the demonstration about the bookshop raid took place. But Kirk decided that it was time to have a go at the mosque.

"You've really got to pick your time," Kirk told Jed. "Some of these Pakis, they know how to defend themselves."

"You think?" Jed said, dismissively.

"Too right I do," Kirk insisted. "Know your enemy. Come on."

They got out of his car, an ancient Ford Cortina with mud splattered over the number plates. They had the blood in paint cans. The idea was to paint slogans on the door, then crowbar their way in, put the rest of the blood over the altar or whatever they had in there, then scarper.

But it didn't work out that way.

Before Kirk had finished painting the first "B" on the mosque wall, there was a yelping noise. Half a dozen tall Asians came running out from what they'd assumed was an abandoned van. Kirk swore. The Asians were blocking the path to his car. He lifted the paint can and tried to throw it at them, succeeded in getting blood all over himself.

"Come on!" Jed called. "Run!"

But it was too late. One of the Asians grabbed Kirk. Jed ran to the far end of the car park. Only when he got there did he realize that the wall was too high to climb over. Three of the Asians, one of them brandishing a knife, were running towards him. The one with the knife spoke in a loud voice.

"Say your prayers, white boy."

From the other end of the car park, he could hear Kirk screaming.

Ben lay on his bed at home in Charlene's arms. When she held him too tight his ribs ached. Charly had come as soon as she could. She had to catch an early train back to London in the morning. It was getting on for midnight, but neither of them were ready to sleep. Instead, they were doing what they'd been doing since she arrived, three hours before. They were talking about their relationship.

"I feel like you've been ... different, Ben. Ever since you finished at Ryton, you've got worse."

"How am I different?"

"More distanced, distracted, more tense ... you

used to have a lovely sense of humour. What happened to it?"

What happened to yours? Ben thought. We're suffering from your stressful job, too. But he knew that this was the wrong time to say it.

"Come to London," she said. "I know you'd get a job. I'd support you until you did."

"On your salary?"

"I'll be fully qualified soon. We'd manage."

Ben squeezed her hand.

"I appreciate what you're offering to do. But I don't want to live in London. And I don't want to leave the force, either."

She stroked his bruised arm.

"This is the second time in a month that you've been beaten up because you're black. If you stay, it won't be the last time."

Ben didn't agree. He tried to keep his voice calm.

"The first time I was unlucky. The second time I was stupid. I won't make the same mistake again."

"And what if the third time you get killed? I'm not waiting around for a knock on the door, Ben. I won't live my life like that."

Anybody who lived with a police officer had to accept that risk, Ben thought. Why wouldn't she?

"No one's forcing you to," Ben told her, gently.

She was crying. He was nearly crying too.

"I don't want to break up with you," Charly said,

looking away from him. "But it seems to be happening."

They had come this far, this quickly. When Charly rushed over this evening, Ben thought that she was playing Florence Nightingale. Instead she was Jezebel.

"Is there somebody else?" he asked, not wanting to know the answer.

"Not really," she said.

Which meant there was. Her eyes stared sadly into his and Ben knew what would happen in the rest of the night. They would talk some more. They would probably make love, very carefully, so as not to hurt him. They might even get a couple of hours' sleep. Then she would go, and they would probably never see each other again.

His ribs might be cracked, but it was his heart that was breaking.

Jan and Baljit were alone in the parade room. Neil was with Ray Willow. Any moment now, he would give the go ahead for Carl to arrest Willow's partner from the pub. Carl was waiting outside this man's house. Jan booked out a car so that she could join Carl and pick the man up. As she was leaving, a report came on the radio about an attack on a mosque. She turned to Baljit. He was busy drawing some kind of diagram which made no sense at all to her.

"Do you want to get in on that?" she asked him.

"The mosque?" he queried. "It's not on our beat."

"I know, but it's near and they'd probably appreciate…"

"…an Asian officer?" Baljit finished her sentence for her. "For your information, Sergeant, I'm a Sikh, not a Muslim. And I'm in the middle of trying to figure out something important."

Jan felt the need to apologize, to get things straight between them, but Carl Price was waiting for her. At this moment, an arrest was more important than good race relations, so she left.

The partner's house was on a tacky side street, the kind which the council cleaning contractors had long since abandoned to dog muck and broken glass. Carl Price was waiting in an alleyway between two sets of terraced houses. Jan turned her lights off as she got into the street, parking a few doors away from the suspect's house. Carl slipped into the seat beside her.

"It's all happening on the Woodborough Road, eh?"

He shouldn't have had his radio on that frequency, but Jan left it. Price got on her nerves. She switched on the radio. They listened to the reports.

"Two white males were apprehended by Asian vigilantes as they approached the mosque. One of these is in custody, waiting to be seen by a doctor. We're still looking for the other: description – late teens, short hair, boots – no tattoos or other markings, medium build. Not believed to be armed. Six Asian males are helping us with our enquiries."

Carl laughed.

"What's so funny?" Jan asked.

"You know what's going to happen, don't you? The six blacks'll get done for assault. The skinhead will probably end up getting money from the criminal compensation board."

"And you think it'd be funny if that happened?"

"They're all as bad as each other, aren't they?" Carl sneered. "Muslims, the National Front – completely barmy."

Jan bit her lip. The course she'd been on was still fresh in her mind. She wanted to give Carl a lecture. But she left it for now. Better to let him talk himself into a hole of his own making. She wished that Neil would get a move on and radio the go ahead.

Ray Willow sat on a fake leather sofa in his dressing-gown. The room was cold and he was shivering. The central heating must have gone off hours before. Neil repeated the question for the third time.

"The man you were sitting next to in the Rose and Crown – Ted Fleming – how well do you know him?"

"I told you," Willow insisted. "I've never met him before tonight. We struck up a conversation, that's all."

"What was the conversation about?"

"Football and … eh … darts."

"Which team does he support, Fleming?"

"I didn't know his name was Fleming."

"That's not what I'm asking you. Which team? You say you were talking about football."

"Man United."

"Are you sure about that?" Neil probed. "You see, I've got someone waking Fleming up this very minute. They'll be asking him the same questions. Which team?"

"He follows Forest too."

Willow was nervous, rattled. He was defensive, but didn't challenge Neil's brusque questions. Neil needed an admission, or something close to one, before he could take Willow to the station, question him properly. He tried to press his advantage, conscious of Carl and Jan, waiting in a cold car.

"You don't know him very well, you say?"

"I said tonight was the first time…"

Neil shook his head.

"Do yourself a favour. You didn't see me in the pub tonight, but I saw you. And I spoke to other people, too. They'd seen you and Ted together before."

"I … I may have…"

Willow didn't know how much Neil knew. And Neil still had an ace card to play.

"It'll be a lot easier," Neil said, in his softest voice, "if you tell me what really happened. I think I know most of it already."

"How ... what?"

"Come on, Mr Willow. Look, if this makes it any easier, it's not you we're after, it's Fleming. I don't know what he did. Maybe he threatened you."

This had no effect.

"Or maybe you had money troubles. Maybe he told you how easy the card con was, offered to split fifty-fifty. You were tempted. It was too hard to resist."

Willow was trying not to say anything, but Neil thought that he could see his head begin, almost imperceptibly, to nod. He pressed his point.

"You knew it was wrong. You made a mistake. Then you reported it, almost immediately after you'd given Fleming the new card. You thought that he hadn't even had time to steal any money yet, that the card would be cancelled. If you tell the court that, they'll be lenient: a fine, a suspended sentence at most. But you have to tell us what you know about Fleming. Was that the way it happened?"

Neil tried to keep the earnest, compassionate expression on his face. Willow was staring at him, almost staring through him. He wanted to confess, Neil knew that.

"Was it?" he repeated, softly.

This time, Willow unmistakably nodded. Then his chin wobbled. Then he began to weep.

"It was just the way you said," he told Neil. "I met him in the pub. He knew I was having trouble with the mortgage payments. He told me he knew a way to make easy money, hundreds. He said he did it all the time."

"OK," Neil said, getting up and handing the man a tissue. "Don't worry. I want you to go upstairs and get dressed, then I'll take you to the station to make a statement. It won't take long."

Ray Willow let Neil guide him out of the room to the stairway in the hall, then, slowly, climbed the stairs. Neil found it perturbing, seeing this man, twice his age, breaking into tears, having to be told what to do. But as soon as he went into the bedroom, to be on the safe side, he radioed Jan. It was quite possible, Neil knew, that Willow would have second thoughts. If he had a phone in his bedroom, he could warn Fleming, tell him to get out of the house before the police got there first. The radio response was immediate.

"OK," Jan said. "Well done. We're going in."

"Edward Fleming, I'm arresting you on suspicion of fraud. You do not have to say anything, but anything you do say may be taken down and used in evidence."

Fleming had nothing to say as they bundled him into the back of the car and took him to the station. Neil was already there, questioning Ray Willow in front of a tape recorder. Baljit, who had helped Neil bring him in, waved hello to Jan as he went back out on patrol. He would be alone again, Jan noted, but it couldn't be helped. Paul Grace appeared as Baljit went out.

"Good work," he told Jan. "Where's PC Foster?"

"Questioning Willow."

"Pass my congratulations on to him. I've rousted a couple of blokes from CID out of their beauty sleep. Keep Fleming on hold until they get here to question him. They're going to be very pleased with tonight's haul."

Jan smiled politely. She hadn't really expected to be allowed to question Fleming. After all, he might turn out to be a big fish, though she doubted it. Nevertheless, she and Carl Price had brought him in. That looked good for them. And Neil had done brilliantly. It wouldn't be long before he found himself in CID, she thought. If he did, she'd miss him.

Jed crouched behind a green wheely-bin. There were four police cars sweeping the area, looking for him. Every so often, Jed heard them pass. They'd taken Kirk, and six Asians – the three who he'd managed to escape from and the three who'd thrashed Kirk. Jed wished that he could drive. He could have got home in Kirk's car, which was still parked outside the mosque. But he had to be back in Nottingham in the morning, for the disciplinary hearing at the youth centre.

The youth centre, that was where he would go. He still had a set of keys, until tomorrow at least, and knew the combination on the alarm, if they hadn't changed it. All he had to do was find his way there. He didn't know the city well, but it couldn't be too far away.

He set off up the hill, hoping that he was going in the right direction. To his left was an area of big houses, with driveways you could duck into. Jed didn't know what it was called, but it was clearly a rich area. Not many Asians could afford to live here. If he heard a police car coming, it would be easy to conceal himself. He walked as fast as he could, keeping in the shadows, wondering about what had happened to Kirk. The police had got there quickly. The Asians wouldn't have had time to do him any real damage, would they? He wondered if Kirk knew that he had got away.

Jed was so busy thinking about the attack on the mosque that he began to lose track of which direction he was going in. There was a roundabout, and he headed along Lucknow Drive. Or was it Lucknow Road? Then he found himself on a road where he'd definitely been before. He found the name plate: Lucknow Avenue. All these roads looked the same to him. He carried on walking, wishing that he had a map, or a compass. He felt like a pillock – getting lost a mere mile from the city centre. But the roads were silent and he was safe, for now at least. Jed carried on, retracing his steps, planning what he would say and do at the hearing tomorrow.

Charlene had dozed off. She lay in the bed, one slender arm stretched around Ben's shoulder. They had resolved nothing between them. Ben couldn't sleep. His back ached, as well as his ribs. He couldn't get comfortable. Maybe he ought to see an osteopath. But that wasn't all that was keeping him awake. He felt angry and confused. If Charly had got that job in Nottingham, none of this need have happened. If he had walked a different way home from work two and a half weeks ago. If…

It was no use. Ben's system was out of whack, partly because of the beating on Saturday and partly because he was geared up to be on nights this week. He should be working now. When he got like this, he was better off getting out of bed, reading, listening to the world service, whatever. Anything was better than staring at the ceiling, thinking dark thoughts, next to a woman who was about to leave him.

Ben got up. Charlene didn't stir. Ben picked up some clothes and went into the living-room. He called this place a flat, rather than a bedsit, but the truth was that the main living space was one big room divided by a partition which separated the narrow sleeping area from the slightly larger area where he kept the TV, his stereo, a sofa and one bookcase. Now he sat on the sofa and dressed. A walk would clear his head, straighten up his back.

Ben put on an anorak and a pair of gloves. Should he leave Charlene a note in case she woke up? Why bother? He let himself out quietly so as not to wake her or the couple in the downstairs flat.

The night was fresh and windy. Clouds scudded across the sky, occasionally revealing a bright, crescent moon. Ben walked up the hill, into the dark, wide roads at the heart of the park. In the distance, he could hear police cars. Anyone seeing him in this rich, tree-lined area would assume that he was there for one purpose: theft. Ben didn't have his warrant card on him. But you couldn't live your life in fear of arrest. That would mean that they'd won.

Ben walked aimlessly along the quiet, moonlit streets. At night, you noticed things you missed in the day, when it was impolite to stare. A house on Richmond Drive had one of the old red phone boxes in the garden. Ben wondered if it worked. On Lucknow Drive, some of the houses were so big that they were practically mansions. One had a satellite dish in its garden so gigantic, it might belong to NASA. A model railway line ran through the grounds. Did the people in these houses inhabit the same world as the people who Ben dealt with in his job? It was hard to fathom. Some of these places not only had burglar alarms, they had security guards, electric gates. They didn't even need to rely on the police, like the rest of society.

As he walked past one, more modest, driveway, Ben heard a scuttling noise. A dog, maybe? But a dog wouldn't have gone quiet on hearing Ben's footsteps. He almost left it. So what if it was a burglar? People around here could afford to lose a few possessions. But it couldn't be much of a burglar. There was no car outside the house, no means of escape unless the thief had a bicycle stashed behind the garden wall. Still, Ben was tempted to leave it. He wasn't on duty, not now.

But duty got the better of him. After walking away so that his footsteps could be heard receding into the distance, Ben crept back towards the house, taking care not to be heard. There was still no sound. Perhaps it had been an animal. Ben waited, pressed against the wall, to see what happened. A few seconds later there was a rustling noise. A head darted out from behind the wall. Its owner couldn't have spotted Ben because he came out a moment later, turned, and headed off in the opposite direction, the one that Ben had come from.

Ben stepped out of the shadows.

"Hold it right there, Jed."

12

It was nearly six. Neil was about to go off duty when DI Greasby came in.

"Just the man I want to see. You got a real result. Well done."

"Thanks," Neil said. "Did Fleming confess to everything?"

"We've cleared up a dozen cases."

"All frauds like this one?"

"He's confessed to one other. The rest were stolen cards. We found plenty of evidence in his flat."

"So, none of your high-tech theories about people counterfeiting cards came true?"

Greasby laughed.

"Old-fashioned theft is a lot easier to prove." He paused. "I'll make sure that my boss drops a line to your boss, praising you for this. If you ever fancy a transfer to us, I'd be happy to put in a word."

"Thanks. I appreciate that."

The inspector left. While Neil got changed, he thought about what Greasby had said. Did Neil want to join CID? He didn't know. He wasn't like Clare, whose only ambition was to be some kind of great detective. But he did enjoy that kind of work. And he was pretty good at interviewing people. When Inspector Grace had him in for a chat recently, they had mainly talked about how Ben was getting on. But Grace had also asked about Neil's career plans. It was too early for him to think about his sergeant's exams, Neil told Grace, but he would be interested in getting into CID or Traffic.

Traffic, Grace told Neil bluntly, was a really plum assignment these days. They had their pick of the high flyers. He'd be lucky to get a chance. Neil understood this. The word "Traffic" was bit of a misnomer. They didn't deal with very many accidents. The people at Traffic wanted to be renamed "Rapid Response Units". That was how they saw themselves: yellow jacketed heroes in unmarked white Carltons, shooting around the city picking off the cream of the cases as soon as they were reported. In CID, on the other hand, you worked more regular hours, and there were plenty of prestige jobs. The work was interesting. You had real continuity on a case, like with this cash card thing. It could be the place for him.

Baljit joined Neil on the steps as he was leaving.

"Well done," he told Neil.

Baljit knew all about the case as he had picked up Neil and Ray Willow earlier.

"Thanks," Neil said. "How was your shift?"

Baljit shrugged.

"It's better working on my own than with PC Price."

"I know how you feel," Neil told him.

"Do you?" Baljit said, in a rather ominous way.

Neil didn't reply directly. Instead he said,

"Look, you've been working here a fortnight and we've hardly had a chat yet. Do you want to get a drink now?"

"I don't drink."

"Neither do I, at this time. I meant a cup of tea, or a cocoa at the caff down the road. Whatever takes your fancy."

Baljit half smiled.

"I appreciate the offer, but I'm tired and I need to stop somewhere on the way home. You know, you're one of the good ones. Some other time, OK?"

"OK," Neil replied, and the two men went their separate ways.

Neil was mystified by Baljit's remarks, but he was ready for bed himself, and let it go.

Jed sat in the office trying to remain alert. He'd only

managed a couple of hours' sleep last night, thanks to getting lost and running into Ben Shipman.

"Jeremy Sutcliffe," the councillor said. "I take it you understand the reason why you were suspended."

"Yeah."

"You are a racist."

"What's wrong with that?" Jed said, defiantly.

"Mr Jagger and Mr Jones gave you the chance to make a fresh start. Instead, you organized Nazi meetings in this building, and circulated racist propaganda amongst the youths who come here."

"That's right."

"You broke our trust."

"If you say so."

The councillor shook his head, as though Jed were the most loathsome creature it had ever been his misfortune to come across. He turned to the chairman.

"Mr Jagger, would you like to ask some questions?"

The lawyer, who had been staring at a sheet of paper, lifted his pencil very slowly but didn't look up. It was as though the very sight of Jed repelled him. As he spoke, Jed tried to meet Jagger's gaze, but saw only bushy, grey eyebrows.

"The actions which have already been described justify your dismissal. But you were also responsible for a brutal assault on a member of the police force."

"We didn't know he was a policeman," Jed protested. "He could have been about to attack us."

Jagger didn't dignify this comment with a response.

"You have not cooperated with the police enquiry by naming your accomplices and almost certainly face charges of assault."

That was the first Jed had heard of that. But he stayed quiet.

"All those matters are for the courts, not for us. However, before we dismiss you, I want to give you a warning."

"Yes, sir."

"If you ever show your face in here again, the police will be called. We don't want you within a mile of these premises. If you have any sense, you'll stay away from this city altogether. Do you understand?"

"Yes, sir."

"Good. Now wait outside while we consider your case."

It was stupid, Jed thought. Jagger had already told him what they were going to do. Unless … unless the whole thing was a show, put on for the benefit of the other two members of the panel. He waited. It wasn't long. Two minutes later, the councillor and Laurie Jones came out.

"He wants you back in there," Jones said.

This time, as he walked in, Jagger met his gaze.

"Shut the door and sit down."

Jed did as he was told. Once the door was closed, the lawyer's voice became warmer.

"You were unlucky," Jagger told him, "that policeman arriving when he did. It should have been a safe time to hold a meeting. I believe the officer was off duty. Not that that makes much difference. You haven't been charged yet?"

Jed shook his head. Jagger handed him a card.

"Here's a lawyer who I suggest you call when they do. Because of my involvement with this centre, it would not be appropriate for me to represent you. I hope you understand that."

"Sure."

"The story will be that you did not know the people who attended the meeting, that you were a pawn of the leading figure – by whom I mean Brig, but you will claim not to know his name – and you did not participate in the kicking that the police constable received. Understood?"

"Yeah."

"Unless you are very unlucky you will receive a fine or community service. The movement will pay your fine for you."

"Thanks."

"Don't thank me. It is I who should be thanking you. That business at the mosque last night – were you involved with that?"

Jed hesitated. He wasn't sure that it was a good

idea to talk about the mosque attack. But he couldn't lie to Jagger.

"Yeah. It was a bit of a cock-up. I scarpered, but they got Kirk."

"Don't worry about Kirk. He was bailed out this morning. The evidence against him is flimsy, to say the least. You'll be pleased to know that he speaks highly of you. He takes full responsibility for last night's mishap. Evidently you went in too early."

"I guess that was it."

Jagger stood up.

"You'll need some more work," he said. "Unfortunately, I can't get you another legitimate job, like this one, until we find out what criminal convictions, if any, you end up with. But you'll need some money to live on."

"I'll get by."

Jagger pulled out his wallet.

"You're a valued member of the organization, Jed, and an intelligent one. I want you to lay off the high profile activity for a few weeks, get involved in fund-raising instead."

Fund-raising? Jed thought. What did he mean? Jumble sales? Street collections? Jagger handed him three twenty pound notes.

"Take this for your expenses."

The lawyer brushed aside Jed's attempts to thank him.

"Stay at home. In the next few days, Brig will get

in touch with you about a way of raising money for the movement."

Jed chanced a question.

"I thought we got plenty of money from European fascist groups?"

Jagger smiled.

"Some, yes. But not as much as we used to. They have heavy demands of their own, and the movement in Britain has let them down too many times in the past. Don't worry. We have other ways of raising funds, and there'll be a good cut in it for you. Brig will be in touch."

"OK," said Jed. "Thanks."

They shook hands.

"Now," said Jagger. "I want you to leave the building very quickly. I'm supposed to have been giving you a lecture about letting me down, and the consequences of getting on the wrong side of the law. Therefore I want you looking angry and depressed. Can you do that?"

"You bet. Give my best to Kirk."

"I will. It may be a long while before we meet again. So, good luck."

"The same to you. Goodbye and ... thanks."

Jed hurried out of the building, feeling lucky.

13

It was the weekend at last. The house Ruth and Clare were going to look round was in Forest Fields. The two girls were on foot, as it was only a ten minute walk from Clare's parents' house. On the way, Ruth asked after Neil.

"I'm going to see him this afternoon when he wakes up. It's his last day on nights, so … if you want to do something later on, give me a ring."

"I'll do that," Ruth said. "How's Ben?"

"You're very interested in him all of a sudden," Clare teased. "He's still off work, but due back next week. Maybe you could take him round a bunch of grapes."

"Don't." Ruth punched her friend lightly on the arm.

"He's split up with his girlfriend," Clare said, with a spark in her eye.

"What?"

Ruth thought that Clare was still teasing her.

"Neil told me last night. We had a meal before his shift. He went round to see Ben yesterday. Ben didn't exactly say that they'd split up, but when Neil asked about it, Ben said that they were giving the relationship a rest. So how about it?"

"How about what?" Ruth said, impatiently.

"Going round to see him. There must be some pretext you could use. Don't you want to know about that skinhead you followed last week?"

"CID don't seem to have done anything about him," Ruth complained.

"But wasn't he one of the ones who beat Ben up?"

"The main one, Ben told me," Ruth said. "I guess you're right. I'll give him a call but … I don't think he fancies me."

"Don't do yourself down," Clare said. "Offer to cook him a meal."

"I can't cook, you know that."

"Then offer to bring round a takeaway. Have a go. Here we are."

It was a street of semi-detached houses, halfway along Gregory Boulevard. Ruth didn't know this area well. It wasn't as near to town as where she was now, but it was close enough, and near the Forest, which was nice to walk through.

"The outside needs painting," Clare commented, as she rang the doorbell.

"You must be Ruth and Clare. I'm Sam. Come in," said the woman who opened the door. She had blonde, frizzy hair and was in her early thirties, Ruth guessed.

"Are the rooms still free?" Ruth asked, as they walked into the wide hallway with its Minton tiled floor. Sam replied in a rush.

"One's empty and Stella's moving out in a fort-night. You did say on the phone that you wanted somewhere in three weeks' time?"

"That's right."

Ruth and Clare answered a few questions about where they were living now. Sam seemed to assume that they were students and neither girl told her otherwise. Then the landlady showed them around.

The empty room was big and airy. The girls nodded appreciatively and then were shown "Stella's room". Furry animals covered the top of a chest of drawers. Ruth hated fake furry animals, but the room was cosy. Though maybe it only seemed cosy because it was filled with feminine stuff, while the other one was empty.

"My bedroom's at the end," Sam explained. "Steve, the other lodger, has the attic room. There's only one bathroom, but there's a separate shower and toilet, so we wouldn't get in each other's way too much."

They were shown these rooms. Downstairs, there was a big, knocked-through living-room and a dining kitchen.

"Of course, you can eat down here, and we all share the living-room."

As they were talking, the back door opened, and someone wheeled a bicycle into the utility room at the back. A dark-haired figure in a denim jacket and jeans walked into the kitchen. He was drop dead gorgeous.

"This is Steve," Sam told them.

"We'll take the rooms," Clare said.

The cards were on the table. The white, virginal plastic with a dark strip across one side looked out of place in Brig's stuffy front room, which was decorated with Nazi memorabilia and racist posters. The only way of telling the cards apart was the number felt-tipped on one side.

"Where do you get them?" Jed asked.

"Ask no questions, get told no lies. Just put them in the right way round and don't let anybody see the card as you're doing it."

"Are you sure that this is safe?" Jed asked Brig.

"Safe as houses. You've just got to remember the rules. Never go to the machines in bank foyers. They have security cameras in there. Never take out more than the card limit in a day. And, as soon as the machine rejects a card, get shot of it, destroy it completely. Never be tempted to give it another go."

"Sounds dead easy."

"Yeah, but remember the other thing. Absolute security. You don't mention this to people in the movement. And you don't get greedy, either. Keep the ten per cent for yourself and put the rest in the safe deposit box."

"How will Jagger know if one of us has been helping ourselves?"

"Oh, he'll know all right, believe me. And never mention his name again. Not even to me. Got that?"

"I've got it."

"Here then."

Brig handed him a slip of paper. On it were five four number codes which went with the cards, and a note of which machines accepted which cards.

"Learn the numbers, then destroy it. All right?"

Jed nodded.

"How long have you been doing this?" he asked Brig.

"None of your business. Oh, one more thing."

"What?"

"If you're caught with them, you bought them off a bloke in a pub, yeah? You'd better make sure that you've got a decent story ready."

"Fair enough."

Jed got out his wallet and picked up the cards.

"No, not in there. People might notice them

when you're paying for something. You've got an inside pocket in that jacket, yeah?"

"Yeah."

"Use that."

Jed began to sweat, not wanting Brig to see what was in his inside pocket. He reached in to unzip it.

"Only take one card out with you at a time," Brig said. "Less risk. Easier to dump if you're followed."

He stared at Jed as he slipped the cards into the pocket.

"That jacket," he said.

"What?"

He was going to frisk him, Jed was sure.

"When you get home, cut a hole in the lining. Keep the cards in there. That's safest."

"OK. Fine."

"Now go through it again for me."

Jed went through everything that he had been told.

"You're a smart lad," Brig said, when he'd finished. "You've got a good future." Then, as Jed was leaving, he added,

"Court case is next week."

"You going to watch it?" Jed asked Brig.

"And risk someone recognizing me? No chance. Nothing to stop you going though. But make sure you haven't got anything on you."

"Got it," Jed said, then got out, as quickly as he could.

* * *

"Did you have to be quite so obvious?" Ruth asked.

"Obvious?" Clare looked puzzled.

"About fancying that bloke."

"I was joking."

"I should hope so. You've got a boyfriend."

"Who I'm very fond of. No. I thought that Steve was your type."

"He's bound to have a girlfriend," Ruth complained. "Maybe he's going out with Sam."

"Oh, dream on," Clare said. "She's at least ten years older than him."

And that doctor you went out with last year," Ruth said. "How much older than you was he?"

"It's different for girls. So tell me," Clare said, changing the subject. "Are you going to call Ben?"

"That's for me to know and you to find out. I'll turn off here," Ruth said as they reached the Boulevard. "I'll catch a bus into town on Mansfield Road."

"OK," Clare said. "I'm off to see Neil. I'll call you later."

Ruth walked on. She was annoyed with Clare, making the decision about the rooms without consulting her. She'd bet that Clare expected to get the bigger of the two rooms, though they hadn't discussed that yet, either. Ruth had liked the house well enough and she didn't want to live on her own for much longer. It would work out cheaper than her bedsit, too. But it was a big decision. She was surprised that Clare could take it in such a casual way.

When she got to the Mansfield Road, she didn't turn right, towards town. She turned left. Clare might be her best friend, but she didn't tell her every little thing. One great advantage of this house could be that it was only ten minutes' walk from Ben Shipman's flat.

Or less. Maybe she was walking quickly, but the journey took only five minutes. Nervously, Ruth rang the doorbell. At first, the house remained silent and Ruth decided that Ben must be out. If he was back at work next week, then he was probably up and about. Then she heard footsteps on the stairs and had the opposite worry. Suppose she had got him out of bed? Should she have brought grapes, as Clare suggested? No, that was silly. When Ben opened the door he was dressed: rather well dressed, in fact, in beige chinos and a yellow polo shirt.

"I hope I'm not disturbing you," Ruth said, awkwardly, "but I was in the area and..."

"Not at all," Ben said. "Come in."

His flat was small but stylish, Ruth thought. She noted the poster of Martin Luther King above the bookcase, the jazz and funk CDs, the absence of a photo of his girlfriend.

"How are you?" she asked.

"Still a bit stiff, but not in pain any more. Ready to go back to work, really."

"Good. I'm glad to hear it."

"Would you like a coffee?"

Ruth was still standing in the doorway of the living-room.

"Er, yes. Thanks."

"Let me take your coat. Have a seat."

She did as he suggested. At least, he doesn't seem uncomfortable that I'm here, she thought. That's a start.

It was proper coffee, made in a cafetière. He had expensive tastes, Ruth thought. He probably picked them up from his girlfriend.

"I really appreciated you taking me to Casualty last week," Ben said. "It was stupid of me not to go earlier."

Ruth smiled sympathetically.

"I came round to see how you were and, well … to find out what's happened about those racists. Did they arrest the lad who worked there?"

"They questioned him, but they haven't charged him yet."

"Why not?"

Ben looked uncomfortable.

"I don't actually remember him hitting me, or kicking me. He'll deny it, of course. I don't want to lie. The others, yes, particularly the one who you spotted and followed. But not the lad."

"Have CID got a name for the big one, with the boot tattoo?"

Ben shook his head.

"The lad who worked there, Jed Sutcliffe, told CID he didn't know any of the names. That's nonsense, of course. The way I figure it, there were half a dozen lads from the estate and this guy was there to recruit them."

"If he's going round recruiting racists, somebody must know who he is," Ruth suggested. "It can't be that hard to find out."

"Maybe you're right," Ben replied. "But you know CID. They only tell you what they think you need to know."

Ruth nodded and they fell into silence. She felt like Ben was being cagey with her, but she didn't know why. Maybe that was his nature, to be secretive. She sipped her coffee. Ben asked after Clare.

"She's fine. We've been looking at a shared house together, off Gregory Boulevard."

"Any good?"

"Really good, yes. We both liked it. The two other people living there seemed nice, too."

"And how did they like the idea of living with two policewomen?"

Ruth hesitated.

"They didn't say what they did and we didn't tell them what we did," she admitted.

They had probably given Steve and Sam the impression that they were students on some kind of sandwich course.

"But, anyway," she went on. "We're moving in when we finish at Ryton, in three weeks."

"Really?"

"You seem surprised?"

"It's only…"

He gave her a cautious look.

"Go on," Ruth urged.

"I got the impression that Neil was hoping Clare would move in with him when he found a house."

Ruth chose her words carefully.

"I don't think that Clare's given Neil that impression."

"I guess you're right," Ben said, thoughtfully. "But then, you never really know what's going on in other people's relationships, do you?"

"No," said Ruth, "you certainly don't."

There was another coffee sipping silence. Ben asked her some polite questions about her week at Ryton. She asked him what he'd been doing in his week off, but he didn't seem terribly keen on telling her. Ruth got a feeling that he was holding things back from her. She was sure that he hadn't told her the full story about Jed Sutcliffe. I'm wasting my time here, Ruth thought. We're acquaintances, colleagues, not potential lovers. There's no spark, no…

"What are you doing tonight?" Ben asked her.

14

"I hope you haven't come back too soon," Jan told Ben when he reported in the parade room on Monday afternoon.

"I'm fine," he assured her. "Where's Neil? It's not like him to be late."

"He's in court. So's Carl. And John's called in sick. I'd like you to partner Baljit today."

"Fine."

Ben nodded at the turbanned officer, who ignored him. What's his problem? Ben wondered. He checked the noticeboard, then collected a radio.

"Did you get anywhere on the cashpoint muggings?" Jan was asking Baljit.

"Not yet," Baljit replied brusquely.

"Do you want to drive, or shall I?" Ben asked, when they were in the car park. He was a probationer.

Baljit wasn't. The more experienced officer made the decisions.

"Whatever you want," Baljit said.

"Normally, I prefer to drive, but I'm still a bit stiff," Ben told Baljit. "Perhaps it'd be better if you…"

"If you're not well," Baljit said testily, "you should stay off work. Why knock yourself out? It's only a job, and not a very good one at that."

Mr Cynical, Ben thought, as Baljit got into the driver's seat.

"What were those cases Jan was asking you about?" Ben enquired, as they set off.

Baljit stared ahead as he replied.

"There've been three muggings at a cashpoint on the edge of the Maynard Estate. The offender's a white teenager who observes the number being typed in, then takes the card and the money. He gets away through the estate. Then, later in the day, he or someone else takes more money out on the card from a different machine, up to its daily limit."

"Got anywhere with it?"

Baljit kept a stony face. He doesn't like to share, Ben thought. Fair enough. I'm only with him for the day. He kept talking, though, trying to break the ice. Eventually, it seemed to work.

"Over there," Baljit said, pulling up on the edge of the Maynard Estate.

"What?"

"That's the machine. I reckon that the mugger keeps watch from the bus shelter fifty yards away. When there's no queue and he sees a likely victim, he goes over, pretends to be waiting to use the machine, watches the number being typed in and memorizes it. Then, he waits until the victim is putting the card away in a purse or wallet and grabs the money as soon as it comes out. He gets the wallet too, if he can, then tears off into the estate."

"Let's have a look," Ben suggested.

Ben watched as Baljit pretended to use the machine. It would be easy enough, Ben saw, to see what numbers were being typed in. That was provided you stood close enough and the machine user didn't hunch their entire body over the keyboard.

"You think it's the same guy every time?" Ben asked.

"I'm sure of it," Baljit told him. "I've got witnesses who've described him. He runs away along the same route each time."

"Then all we need is a name," Ben said.

Baljit smiled.

"I know the name, too," he told Ben proudly. "All I need now is to catch him at it."

In the car, Baljit showed Ben a map he'd made of the estate, with the route taken by the mugger, crossed at different points where witnesses had observed him running away. The route tailed off in the heart of the estate.

"What do you assume from that?" Baljit asked.

"That he lives there?" Ben suggested.

"Close. His girlfriend does. An older woman, known drug dealer called Denise Carr. I've seen the suspect leaving there several times."

"What's his name?"

Baljit didn't reply.

"Why haven't you gone in there?" Ben wanted to know.

"For what? A few grammes of crack? I need to catch him with the money and the card on him, or there'll be no evidence. So, next time a mugging's radioed in, I go straight to the house, wait for him."

"Sounds fine," Ben told him, "except for one little thing."

"Yes?"

"What if the next mugging takes place during another shift?"

Baljit shrugged.

"Then I wait for the one after."

"You can't do that!" Ben protested. "You'd be allowing crimes to happen. You're a police officer, not the Lone Ranger."

Baljit gave him a deep, sad look. Then he reached into the inside pocket of his jacket. He pulled out a white envelope. Inspector Grace's name was written on it.

"Know what this is?" Baljit asked.

Ben shook his head.

"It's my resignation. I typed it at the weekend. As soon as I've nailed this mugger, I'm going to hand it in. I'm owed a few weeks' holiday so I don't need to serve out my notice period. You won't see me for dust."

"Why?"

"How long have you been on the job?" Baljit asked. "A year?"

"Fifteen months."

"I've been doing it twice as long. After fifteen months, I was still telling myself what you're telling yourself now. That it'll get easier, that I ought to be able to shrug it off, that all I have to do is prove myself and I'll be treated as an equal. Sound familiar?"

"I know what you're talking about," Ben said.

"I'm talking about being ignored, about never getting a regular partner, about never getting the back-up you need, about getting luke-warm assessments so that you only just pass your probation and everyone assumes that you're not good enough. They think that you only got through because of the colour of your skin. I'm not talking about being called a wog, or a nig-nog, but that happens as well. Are you trying to say you haven't had it too?"

Ben thought back over his experiences of the last few weeks.

"Individual racism, yes. Institutional racism, not yet."

"It's there," Baljit told him. "Believe me. It might not be as bad for you. People of Afro-Caribbean descent aren't hated as much, unless they've got dreadlocks. You get a good image in the movies, on TV – hard men. My people get taunted as religious fanatics, only fit to work late in corner shops. But I'm warning you, when push comes to shove, *you're not one of them* and they'll hate you for it."

"Some of them, maybe," Ben replied, thoughtfully. "Not all."

"Enough to make the difference," Baljit argued, angrily. "In my old division, I had a tough time. I was glad to get the temporary transfer here. Inspector Grace told me that if my face fitted, I could stay on. But if you're not white, your face never really fits. I've never had a regular partner. They sent Jan Hunt on a race awareness course. She came back breathing white guilt and let me do exactly what I want. You think that helps me?"

"Maybe she doesn't know how to help you," Ben told Baljit. "Maybe your anger's scaring her off."

"At least she stopped partnering me with that evil sod, Price."

Baljit told Ben about some of the barbed comments that Carl Price had made during their two days working together.

"Did you put a complaint in?" Ben asked.

"The week I arrived?" Baljit laughed bitterly. "That would have looked really good, wouldn't it?

No, I didn't put a complaint in, but I made up my mind to leave."

"What will you do instead?"

"Something practical," Baljit said, with an edge in his voice. "And I'm not talking about opening a newsagent's."

A call came in on the radio.

"Mugging at the cash machine on the edge of the Maynard Estate."

Ben reached out to press the button and respond.

"Stop!" Baljit told him.

Baljit was accelerating but he didn't have the lights or the siren on.

"Why?" Ben asked.

"We'll let another car deal with the victim. We're going to intercept the offender as he goes into Denise Carr's house. His name's Robert Hamill."

"Shouldn't we radio in what we're doing?"

"No. Carr might well have a scanner. We don't want her prepared for us."

They pulled up at some garages just inside the estate. You couldn't drive into the middle of Maynard, as it was pedestrian only. Ben had never done this beat, and didn't really know his way around. But Baljit, who had only been working this beat for three weeks, knew exactly where to go.

"Follow me!" Baljit said. "Hurry!"

Ben had trouble keeping up with Baljit. His chest was on fire. Maybe the Sikh officer had been right before. Maybe he had returned to work too quickly.

"This way."

They charged down an alleyway. At the end of it, Baljit poked his head round the corner.

"He's not here yet," he hissed to Ben. "Get your breath back, but have your truncheon ready."

Ben leant against the brick wall and drew his truncheon. He could hear nothing. Suppose Baljit had got it wrong? This could turn into an embarrassing situation.

But then he heard them, rapid footsteps, coming their way.

"Stay right here," Baljit whispered. "We want to get him at the precise moment she lets him in. That way, we'll have evidence against both of them."

The footsteps grew closer, then stopped. There was the click of a door beginning to open.

"Now!" Baljit whispered.

They whipped round the corner as the door began to close behind the mugger. Baljit barged it back open.

"Robert Hamill, I'm arresting you in connection with an assault and robbery which took place a few minutes ago. You do not have to say anything but anything you do say…"

Denise Carr began to swear at them. Hamill tried to barge his way past Baljit, only to find Ben waiting for him. The two officers handcuffed the mugger, but Ben kept his eye on the woman. Her hands were behind her back. The swearing was intended to distract them, Ben realized. She had something on her. Was it only drugs or...

"Where are you going?" he asked, as she made her move.

"I need the loo."

"You'll have to wait until we can get a female officer here to search you."

"Search me for what? You..."

She began to swear again. Now they had Hamill secured.

"Turn round."

Baljit was radioing in the arrest. Jan Hunt was on her way, but when Ben saw the bulge in the back of Carr's jeans he realized that a strip search wasn't going to be necessary.

"Take the card out of your back pocket, Ms Carr."

Sneering, she did as he instructed. Hamill must have handed it to her the moment he got in through the door.

"And the money too."

"You can't prove..."

"Maybe we can, maybe we can't," Ben said, taking the crisp ten pound notes which had been withdrawn from the cashpoint less than ten minutes before. "Denise Carr, I'm arresting you for receiving stolen goods. You do not have to say anything, but anything you do say may be taken down..."

Outside, in the estate, people were gathering

round, watching the live show. Ben could hear people running. They'd be other officers who'd heard them on the radio, coming to give support. But it was all over bar Denise Carr's shouting. Ben took in the look of satisfaction on Baljit's face.

"Still sure you want to resign?" Ben asked him.

15

It was the day of the bookshop raid trial. Ruth didn't have to be in court until the afternoon so she drove over from Ryton in the morning. She got to Wellington Square at twelve and checked the mail in her bedsit. There were no invitations to the ball, no warm, news-filled letters from old friends, only an electricity bill and a note from her mum, pointing out that she'd forgotten Dad's birthday.

Ruth freshened up and walked into town, thinking about the afternoon ahead. She had never testified in a court before, but she had had practice in role play exercises at Ryton. The prospect didn't scare her. She was early. That was one of her hang-ups, she decided. She was always too keen, too eager. It made people value her less. When it came to Ben Shipman, she should be careful not to push things. Let him make the running. But some things were easier thought than done.

On Saturday night, they'd had a nice time. They'd talked, had a meal, a couple of drinks, talked some more. The more Ruth got to know Ben the more she liked him, and lusted after him. But there'd been no fireworks between them. The evening ended with a handshake, not a kiss. Ruth still wasn't sure where they stood. Maybe he just wanted to be friends. But it never worked that way.

To kill time, she went to the bookshop where the attack had taken place. She didn't recognize the workers who were on today. But then, the ones she knew from before would be in court. On the accommodation board, Sam's card was still up. Ruth took it down and handed it in at the counter.

"This is out of date. The rooms are gone."

The woman behind the counter thanked her. Ruth was about to leave when she saw a magazine on the counter, one she hadn't noticed before: *Searchlight*. It described itself as "The International Anti-Fascist Monthly". There were articles about neo-Nazi activities all over Europe, but mainly in England. There were numerous photographs identifying known racist thugs.

"Have you got any more of these?" she asked the shop worker.

"There are some back issues on the rack over there."

Ruth bought four copies. She could look through them while she was waiting to give evidence.

It was a long wait. There were eleven defendants (the young one, Jed, having been let off with a caution). They sat in the dock, burly figures, uneasily dressed in suits or sports jackets. They might be going to a wedding or a job interview. Their barrister was anxious to show that they had done nothing serious. They had gone into a bookshop where they weren't welcome. It would be hard to prove that any of them were guilty of assault. The defence were willing to admit to "threatening behaviour", but not the more serious charge, "affray".

Ruth sat on the beige covered benches outside the courtroom, next to two of the other witnesses due to appear that afternoon. The walls were painted cream, like a hotel lobby, but the atmosphere was intimidating. It didn't encourage conversation. Ruth got out her magazines and flicked through them. At first she was sickened by the endless array of racist assaults, arson, even killings. Yet after a while, they seemed to blend into one. There were too many to get angry about. She ended up feeling numb.

Her main reason for buying the magazines was the photographs. At first, the skinheads all seemed to look the same. But Ruth had seen the one with the boot tattooed across his forehead twice now. She would recognize him if she saw him again, here, or in the flesh. Nobody else had identified him clearly, not even Ben. He was guilty of at least two assaults, but she had no idea of his name, or where he came from. All she knew was what he looked like, and that he had a bank account with a "Link" machine cash card, the same as her own.

Ruth went through each magazine twice. He wasn't there. It was disappointing, but Ruth guessed that, if he had been in *Searchlight,* one of the shop workers would have spotted him already. The cleverest Nazis, one of the articles pointed out, avoided having their photograph taken at all times. It warned against letting them see you with a camera to hand, as it could easily provoke an attack. If you were lucky it would only be your camera which they smashed up.

There was one photograph which did interest Ruth, though. It showed Kirk Hepton, the racist who'd been arrested for an attack on a mosque in Nottingham, a wiry, demented-looking man. His partner in the attack got away, the article said. Ruth wondered if he was the man who she was after.

She wasn't called until four. Ruth was beginning to think that she'd have to return tomorrow and miss another day's training. In the modern courtroom, she recognized the solicitor, Jagger, sitting smugly behind the defendants' barrister. The prosecution barrister was much younger. On the public benches sat Jed, the youth involved in the attack on Ben.

Ruth gave her name and, when asked her occupation, said "trainee police officer".

"But you were in the shop in a private capacity, is that right, PC Clarke?"

Ruth noted the way that the prosecution barrister used her rank to give her more credibility.

"Yes, that's right. I went in to buy a book."

She described the attack in as much detail as she could muster. Ruth knew the law of affray. She'd read it up. The prosecution had to show that a person of "reasonable firmness" was in fear of violence to themselves.

"And what did you do while this was going on?"

"There were so many of them. There was nowhere to hide. I stood back, hoping that I wouldn't get hit."

"You were afraid?"

"Very afraid, yes. I felt like any of them could have struck me at any time. I counted myself lucky to escape unscathed."

"Thank you, officer."

Ruth blinked. It had gone by so quickly. But then the defence barrister stood up.

"You weren't assaulted, were you, officer?"

"No. I…"

"In fact, you haven't identified any of the defendants as being involved in acts of violence on the people in the shop, have you?"

"No, but I was afraid that…"

"In fact, all you really saw was a bunch of high-spirited men having a bit of fun which got out of hand?"

"That's ridiculous!" Ruth protested. "They knew exactly what they were doing. They were trying to intimidate people like me, stop them from using the shop. I'm sure that they wanted to close it down if they could. It was a violent assault, not a 'bit of fun'."

"But none of the men who committed this so-called violence are in court today, are they?"

"I can't be sure which ones..."

Ruth's voice trailed off.

"Thank you," the barrister said. "No further questions."

Jan knew that something was going on when Baljit ignored her on leaving Paul Grace's office.

"John's waiting for you," she said. "He..."

A moment later, Grace came out and summoned her. He held a letter in his hands.

"Read this."

Jan scanned the white sheet. It only took her a second to see what it was: a letter of resignation. But it was also more than that. She read the second paragraph carefully.

"I believed the rhetoric about equality of opportunity in the modern police force. I was wrong. The top ranks may adopt admirable statements of principle, but racial prejudice is endemic elsewhere, contaminating all

relationships and stifling career prospects. I have never felt so isolated as when doing this job. I do not know which was worse: the outright racial taunts from the minority or the indifference to racial equality from the majority. I can take it no longer."

"It's quite an indictment," Jan said.

"Quite," Paul Grace agreed, in a dry voice.

Just like Baljit, she was thinking, to use lots of big words to make his case, when small ones would have been more effective. His problem was that he tried too hard. But she said none of this. Most of what he said was true. She couldn't argue with that.

"I did try, sir," she said. "I put him in for a commendation after the arrest yesterday. But he had bad luck with partners. And he was hard to get close to … there's always this big chip on his shoulder."

"It sounds to me like there was a reason for the chip on his shoulder," Grace lectured Jan. "Didn't that course I sent you on teach you anything?"

Jan knew when to keep silent and this was one of those times. Even so, it wasn't comfortable, having someone five years younger than you handing out a bollocking which you knew you deserved.

"I'm not going to formally reprimand you, Sergeant," Grace went on. "In PC Singh's case, most of the damage was done before he got here. He saw this shift as the police force's last chance to prove itself. We didn't take that chance. I hold you responsible for that."

"Yes, sir."

"I asked PC Singh for specific complaints about any officers on this shift. He only named one, PC Price. Even then, he refused to make a formal complaint about him. Nevertheless, Price's transfer here was always temporary. I'm sending him back where he came from. Let them sort out their own bad apples."

"That's fine by me, sir."

"You don't have any choice in the matter," Grace told her. "What it also means is that you'll be two officers short until Clare Coppola returns to the shift. Don't expect to get a quick replacement."

"No, sir."

"And don't think that this will be forgotten. Singh's sent a copy of his resignation letter to the Chief Constable, and doubtless he's sent one to the Commission for Racial Equality, too. I'll have some explaining to do, and you'll have to make sure that nothing like this happens on your shift again, or you won't be keeping those sergeant's stripes."

"I understand, sir."

"All right. Now get out of here."

Jan left, bristling beneath her uniform. She felt like crying, but two of the men on her shift were sitting in the parade room, sipping coffee and updating their notebooks. She had to keep face.

"What's happened to Baljit, Sarge?" John Farraday asked.

"He's quit the force."

Ben Shipman didn't look surprised. Jan thought for a moment.

"Neil's in court again, isn't he? You two better go out together. No, on second thoughts, I'll go out with Ben. You hold the fort here, John. All right?"

"Fine by me."

"Ready?" she said to Ben.

"Let's go."

"You drive," Jan told Ben when they got to the car.

He took the keys from her.

"Are you all right, Sarge? You look a bit pale."

"Give me a moment or two, will you?"

Ben set off, at a steady pace, keeping a discreet silence. His concern touched Jan. She wanted to talk to him. At first, she hadn't liked the black officer much, but that had passed. Did he like her? He respected her, she knew that. But would he tell her what she wanted to find out?

"Did you know about Baljit?" she asked Ben, after a few minutes.

"He told me yesterday."

"Did you try and argue him out of it?"

"A little. He'd obviously made up his mind already."

"Do you think he was right?"

Ben shrugged.

"It's not a black and white situation, is it?"

"I thought that was exactly what it was."

Ben laughed in a way which indicated that the joke wasn't funny. Then he replied.

"What I mean is – if Baljit experienced the degree of racism he says he did, then he was right to go. I'm not him. I can't say what I'd have done in the same situation."

"What about you? Have you experienced any direct racism in the force?"

"Apart from being beaten up by CID, you mean?" Ben said, sarcastically. Then he went on in a more matter of fact way.

"It depends what you mean by direct racism. I hear comments, but they aren't addressed directly at me. But I'm much taller than Baljit. I don't wear a turban. I'm Jamaican. Jamaicans have a tough reputation. Baljit thought that those things made a difference. He was probably right."

"What about me?" Jan asked him. "Do I treat you fairly?"

They were in heavy, home-time traffic. Ben pulled the car over into a side road. Then he turned round to look at her.

"You're asking me to tell you if I think you're a racist?" he asked.

His tone was one of mild disbelief. Jan wondered again if he liked her enough to be frank.

"Yes. I guess so," she replied.

"Is this because you dropped me as a partner last year?"

Jan nodded slowly.

"I got the impression..." Ben began hesitantly, "...that you didn't like me much."

Jan said nothing.

"But that was OK," Ben went on, "because I didn't like you much either."

Jan forced a fake smile.

"I like you more now," Ben said.

"I like you more too."

Ben nodded, embarrassed, then stared ahead of him before he went on.

"But as to why you didn't like me in the first place, I didn't think that it was racial prejudice."

Jan breathed a sigh of relief.

"Do you want me to tell the inspector that?" Ben asked. "Would it help?"

"I don't think it's necessary," Jan said.

There was a long silence.

"You know what the worst thing is," Ben said, "about being black in this job?"

"No," Jan said. "What?"

She thought that he was going to tell a joke, but when she looked at his face it was serious.

"Whether you're black or white, you want to ignore the whole race thing, to act as though it isn't there, to be equals, professionals, doing a job. But if you're black, you can't. It's always there."

Ben paused and stared straight ahead, speaking slowly.

"Probably, most of the time, it isn't a factor at all, but you never know. You miss a promotion. Your mentor requests a new tutee. The Chief Inspector doesn't invite you to his house for dinner. Probably it has nothing to do with racial prejudice, but maybe it does. *And you never know*. You can never be sure. Do you understand me?"

"Yes," said Jan, feeling, for the first time, that she did.

Ben put the car back into gear.

"That's the worst thing," he said.

16

"These are foolish young men," the defence counsel said, in his closing speech, "who did a stupid thing. They hold views which are abhorrent to civilized society. But they are not a threat, not a serious menace to society. And to treat them as such would be to become part of the pathetic paranoia put forward by the prosecution. Let them go. They have learnt their lesson."

Ben sat in the public gallery, listening. He was here for two reasons. The first was that he wanted to know the outcome of the trial. He was having a drink with Ruth after work tonight and she would want to know all about it. The other was that Ruth had rung him on Tuesday evening. She told Ben that Jed Sutcliffe had been in court, watching. Ben needed to talk to Jed. They had a deal. The young skinhead had promised to get in touch, but, so far, he hadn't. Now he was sitting in the row behind Ben, but Ben couldn't talk to him yet, not here. It would have to be later, when the judge had finished his summing-up.

The summing-up seemed to favour the defence more than the prosecution, but Ben couldn't be sure. He hadn't attended many court cases. When it was over, and the defendants were taken out, Ben waited for the solicitor, Jagger, to leave the room. Then he turned to Jed.

"Why haven't you called me? We had an agreement."

"I know," Jed said, "but I'm not ready yet."

"Why not?"

"Something else has happened. It's too big for you. I can't explain. Soon, I promise."

"All I have to do," Ben warned him, "is to tell Central Division that you were the other person involved in the mosque attack. You'd be in real trouble."

"Ah, but you wouldn't do that, would you?" Jed goaded him. "Because then you'd have to explain why you didn't report it earlier."

He had a point, Ben realized.

"All rise."

Astonishingly, the jury had returned already. They had been out for less than ten minutes. Two minutes later, the skinheads were back in the dock, and the foreman was reading the jury's unanimous verdict. It was one word, repeated again and again and again.

"On the charge of affray, how do you find the defendant?"

"Guilty."

Ben felt a rush of satisfaction. It wasn't to last for very long.

Detective Inspector Greasby was waiting for Neil when he came on shift.

"Thought you'd like to know," he told Neil. "The cashpoint operation's over."

"Already?"

Neil had expected the operation to last for months, not weeks.

"Was it a success?" he asked.

"We won't know that until all the cases have come to court. If you ask me, it's political. We've got a few results across the country, all of them down to fraud or theft. That was the result the banks wanted to hear. It puts them in the clear. No ghosts in the machine, making phantom withdrawals, no crime by bank staff, only dishonest customers."

"Do you believe that?"

Greasby raised his eyebrows.

"Ours not to reason why…"

"Yeah," said Neil. "I guess…"

Ben, who was listening, asked,

"What if more cases come to light?"

"They get treated in the normal way," Greasby told him. "But you know how it is with card crime – intensive investigation, difficult to prove. You have to have cast-iron evidence to get a conviction. Not very cost efficient." He turned to Neil. "That's why Fleming was such a good collar. Willow's confession will put him away for a long slot."

He stood.

"Anyway, I just thought you'd like to know. And remember what I said, there are some attachments to CID coming up in the spring. If you fancy one, I'll put in a word."

"Thanks," Neil said. "I'll think about it."

"You're flavour of the month," Ben said, when Greasby had gone. "Are you going to have a go at CID?"

"It might be a bit early," Neil said. "I dunno. Do you fancy a drink after work tonight? I could do with talking it through."

He meant with someone other than Clare. She would urge him to go for it. His girlfriend wasn't looking forward to being on the same shift as him again.

"Not tonight," Ben replied. "I'm meeting Ruth."

"Aah," said Neil. "Anything going on there?"

"Not the way you mean," Ben told him. "Just friends."

Neil smiled like he'd heard that one before. Ben looked embarrassed.

"All right," he told Neil. "I like her. But she knows the score. After Charlene, I'm in no hurry to get burned again."

Clare had given Neil the impression that Ruth was rather keener than Ben said, but he changed the subject.

"That reminds me," Neil told Ben, "when I was in court the other day, I could have sworn I saw Charlene, with one of the solicitors. Did she have a job on in Nottingham?"

"I wouldn't know," Ben told him. "I don't want to know."

"Sorry I brought it up," Neil told him, and quickly changed the subject again.

Ruth got back from Ryton at eight, had a bath, then ironed a blouse and skirt to wear for Ben. He was joining her when he came off duty, at ten. They'd arranged to meet in the Sir John Borlace Warren, a pub which was only two minutes' walk away. It was still cold, but Ruth felt she could get away with a skirt. She wanted him to see that she had good legs.

When she'd finished ironing, still in her dressing-gown, Ruth tidied the flat. She hoovered, put fresh sheets on the bed, a bottle of white wine in the fridge. Maybe she'd be able to persuade him to come back afterwards. You never knew. She picked a couple of tapes which she thought would appeal to Ben, and stuck them by the machine. One was a compilation of soul ballads, the other a jazz "Best of" by somebody called Dexter Gordon. She'd borrowed it from the library after seeing a CD by Gordon at Ben's flat. Hopefully, if he noticed, he'd be flattered, wouldn't think that she was trying too hard.

When she was dressed and perfumed it was still only half past nine. Ruth sat down and made herself watch Cheers before she went out. There was no fun in being in a busy pub on your own. Then she changed channels to the News at Ten and watched the headlines, half expecting the verdict in the bookshop trial to be on. But the story wasn't big enough. If the jury had reached a verdict, it would be lucky to make the local news.

The time reached five past ten. The earliest Ben could make it to the pub would be ten past. Ruth put her coat on and did her best to walk there very slowly. She passed Scruffy Murphy's and wondered whether she should have suggested a meal instead. But Ben never seemed to eat much. He was very tall and slim. Clare reckoned that he worked out a lot. Ruth hoped he wouldn't be late.

When she got to the bar he was already there, ordering a pint.

"I hope I haven't kept you waiting," she said.

"Just arrived. Vodka and orange?"

She nodded. Soon they were sitting in a private corner where a space had miraculously appeared. Ruth felt lucky.

"Did you hear the verdict?" Ben asked her.

"No. What happened?"

"They were all found guilty of affray."

"That's brilliant," Ruth told him, chirpily. "Isn't it?"

Ben didn't look too pleased.

"You haven't heard the sentence," he said.

Ruth thought.

"Affray – the maximum for that's three years, isn't it? I don't suppose they got that much. Eighteen months each?"

Ben shook his head.

"A year? Six months?"

His head kept shaking.

"How much?" Ruth insisted on knowing.

"Community service. Sixty hours each."

"Sixty hours! It took more time than that to fix up the bookshop." Ruth found herself getting very angry. "That's ridiculous. They really scared me, you know. And that poor woman in the wheelchair."

"There's still a chance of getting someone for that."

"The bloke with the boot on his head? I doubt it."

"I might have a lead," Ben told her.

"What?"

"I can't talk about it in here."

That was her cue, Ruth realized. She had to take it.

"My flat's just round the corner. We could go

there if you like. There's probably some wine in the fridge."

Ben looked slightly surprised.

"I thought you lived near me?"

Ruth smiled slyly. This was cards on the table time.

"I only said that to have an excuse to give you a lift home."

Ben smiled back.

"But I was with Charlene then."

"I know," Ruth told him. "Anyway, never mind. You're not with Charlene now, are you?"

"No," said Ben, downing his pint thirstily. "I guess I'm not."

As they made the short walk from Canning Circus to Wellington Square, Ben slotted his arm into hers. *This is really happening*, Ruth told herself. *We're beginning to get somewhere.*

"What's that?" Ben asked, as she opened the door.

A red sheet of A4 paper poked out from the letterbox, with Ruth's name on it.

DEMONSTRATE!

The sentences passed on the racists convicted of the bookshop attack last month were offensive and obscene. We need to show that the people of Nottingham won't tolerate racism. A demonstration has been called, meeting on the Forest at ten thirty tomorrow (Saturday) and marching into town at eleven. Please attend if you can. If you know of anybody who feels as you do who is not on the bookshop's mailing list, please contact them, telling them about tomorrow's demonstration.

BLACK AND WHITE UNITE AND FIGHT!

"Are you going to go?" Ben asked Ruth.

"Of course I am. Are you?"

"I don't know," he told her, as they climbed the stairs together. "It probably counts as a political demonstration, which we're not meant to get involved with."

"Racism isn't a political issue," Ruth told him. "It's a moral one. The police force oppose racism, officially at least. How could they censure an officer for going on a march?"

"It's been called at such short notice that they probably haven't got police permission," Ben said, hesitantly. "And there's a danger of violence, too. It might not be wise to go."

"You're very cautious, aren't you?" Ruth challenged him. "Well, I'm not a full time police officer yet. I'm still a student, for another fortnight. And I'm going to it. In fact, I think I'll ring Clare, tell her about it too. Why don't you make yourself useful, open the wine?"

Ben did as he was told. Ruth hoped that she hadn't come on too strong with him. Clare wasn't home. She was out with Neil. But her father, Nick, promised to give her a message. When Ruth came back from the phone in the downstairs hallway, Ben had poured two glasses of wine and was sitting on the sofa, next to the electric fire. Ruth took a deep breath and sat down next to him.

"What was it you were going to tell me about?" she asked him.

He told her. When he'd finished, she was impressed.

"And no one at the station knows anything about this?" she asked.

He shook his head.

"It's incredible," she told him, "but can you prove any of it?"

"I can't do anything," Ben told her. "It's up to Jed Sutcliffe. He hinted that he might have something else, too. Something even bigger. Hopefully, he'll have contacted me tonight. I left my answering machine on."

Ruth got them some more wine.

"I'm sure that any messages will wait till tomorrow," she told him, moving a little closer on the settee.

Ben smiled and put a friendly arm around her shoulder.

"I'm sure you're right," he said.

17

Jed made several phone calls. Finally, he rang the policeman again, but got the machine. He didn't like talking into machines. Suppose the tape got into the wrong hands? It was time for him to get the bus, anyway. Today was what the last six months had been leading up to. A spontaneous demonstration played right into the fascists' hands. The police wouldn't have time to prepare a decent battle plan. They might even try to ban it, which would escalate matters further.

Then there were the demonstrators. The lefties were the sort of people who couldn't organize the proverbial party in a brewery. They certainly wouldn't have time to organize decent security or look-outs. Whereas Brig's group had been planning this ruckus for weeks. They knew that there would be a demonstration after the trial. As soon as they found out which judge was trying the case, they even knew that the sentences would be light. They didn't know the route, but they could have a good guess, and prepare contingency plans. They were confident. The sentences yesterday had been a kind of victory, but they were only the appetizer. Today was the main meal.

Ben dressed guiltily and splashed cold water on his stubble. He'd shave at home. He'd have to jog there, or catch a bus into town and back out again, which would take as long. Days like this, he wished he had a car.

"Can I give you a lift?" Ruth offered, as she stood there in her silk dressing-gown.

"You need to get ready for your demonstration."

"It's only five minutes' walk from your place to the Forest," Ruth told him. "I can leave the car there."

Then she'd have an excuse to come back and see him later. Ben was tempted, but he was also confused.

"Oh, stop looking so shifty and finish your tea," Ruth told him. "We said last night – *no commitments.* I'm offering you a lift home. No strings attached."

"Thanks," Ben told her. "I'll take you up on it."

*   *   *

Ten minutes later they were in the car. Ruth was wearing a duffle-coat and jeans. She looked like a student. Ben knew that he ought to be going on this demonstration, too. He admired the way that Ruth brushed aside his objections the night before. As she parked her VW outside his flat, he felt an urge to go with her. To hell with the guidelines! Ruth was right. The force would be far too embarrassed to discipline a black officer for attending an anti-racist march.

"Maybe I'll see you later," Ruth said, tentatively, as they stood outside his flat. "Is it OK if I call by when I come back for the car?"

"Of course it is," Ben said, surprised at her sudden timidity. He kissed her cheek. "Thanks for last night," he said. "You made me feel a lot better about myself."

"You made me feel a lot better about myself, too."

He thought that she was going to kiss him properly, and he would have liked that, but, instead, she gave him a little shy smile then turned away to walk down the hill. She was early. He could have invited her in for coffee. He could go with her. But he had always been a coward, in matters of the heart, had always let the woman make the running. He wasn't about to become any more decisive now.

The green light on his answering machine gave a double flash every five seconds. That meant there were two messages. The first was from Inspector Grace.

"Ben, there's a demonstration taking place on the Forest today and the Chief Super says we've got to allow it to go ahead. The march kicks off at ten-thirty and I'm desperate for officers. If you're able to put in the overtime, give the station a call and I'll make sure a car picks you up."

Ben thought about it, but not for long. He wanted to be at that demonstration. He needed to be. And if anything went wrong, it would help if he was in uniform.

He hoped that the second message would be from Jed, but it wasn't. The next voice on the tape was Charlene's. Her voice was girlish, exhilarated.

"Darling, it's me! I'm sorry I've been so snotty with you recently. Guess what? I've just got some marvellous news. I didn't tell you, but I had my interview for the job in Nottingham this week. I just opened my mail and *I got it!* I start next month. Isn't that amazing? I'm sorry I came on so heavy with you about your job. I gave you a tough time, but things are going to look up now. Give me a ring and I'll get on a train. We could start looking for flats. I'm so excited. Please, call me soon. Love you. 'Bye."

Ben slowly shook his head from side to side. Then he rang the station.

"Inspector? It's Ben. I'm coming in."

* * *

"Whichever way they go, they've got to pass here. That's where we take them."

"But it's right by the Central Police Station," one of the skins protested.

"That's the beauty of it," Brig told him. "They won't be expecting it. We pick off the tail of the march, and by the time the front end's sussed what's going on, we're gone, into the Victoria Centre at the busiest time of day. They'll never catch us."

"What about the police presence?" Jed asked.

"Back end of the march. Maximum, two officers. Probably one. Jed, your job will be to take him out as soon as we attack."

"*Take him out?*"

Brig gave an evil smile.

"Grab his radio, that's all. You got a knife?"

"Yeah."

"Cut the cord or just yank it off him, whatever. If there's two of them, Mick'll get the other one. Right, Mick?"

"Right."

Brig smiled.

"This is going to be our biggest victory since Kirk organized the do in Rotherham. Bigger, if we're lucky. But don't get carried away. As soon as you hear the whistle, leg it. Everyone know the escape route?"

"This alley behind the WEA," Jed said. "You are sure that it'll be clear?"

174

"I checked it last week," Brig told him.

"Why don't I double check it now?" Jed suggested.

"Good idea. Off you go then. Be quick."

Jed hurried to the nearest phone box. He rang one number, and told the person at the other end what he'd just found out. Then he rang Ben Shipman. This time, the officer was in. Five minutes later, Jed was back with the rest of the gang, impatiently waiting for the action to begin.

Ruth walked slowly to the Forest, carefully crossing the roundabout by Sherwood Rise on to Gregory Boulevard. The day was wet. A white mist hung over the Forest. Countless pigeons scoured its green fields for anything they could eat. A bunch of demonstrators were crossing the road with a long white banner drooping between them. Ruth couldn't read the words on it. As the group reached the other side, the pigeons, as one, took flight. For a moment, they became a vast, white umbrella, then they were gone, scattered into the white mist of the morning.

It began to rain heavily. Ruth noticed a figure she recognized walking towards her. They met up at the pedestrian crossing.

"Clare! You got my message."

"Of course I did. I rang you at home a quarter of an hour ago so that we could arrange to meet. You'd already left, so I came straight out. But why are you coming from that direction?"

Ruth blushed.

"I … eh, gave Ben a lift home."

Clare smiled cheekily.

"Last night or this morning?"

"What difference does it make?"

"Not a lot, I guess."

The two girls walked across the wet grass towards the knoll of demonstrators.

"So are you going to tell me about this of your own accord or do I have to pump you for information?" Clare asked in the voice she used for detective role play in training.

"You can pump me for information when we're driving back to Ryton on Monday," Ruth told her. "Who knows? There might be more to tell by then."

She certainly hoped so.

One of the workers from the shop greeted Ruth.

"Are you in the police force too?" he asked Clare. She nodded.

"Makes a change," he commented, "having you on the inside as well as the outside."

Ruth smiled awkwardly as he walked off.

"I wasn't sure you'd come," she said to Clare.

Clare seemed surprised.

"I've been on marches against racism before," she told Ruth, "when I was a student in Manchester. We took a coach to a TUC march in London, too."

"Really?"

Ruth was impressed. It would never have occurred to her to go on such a march if she hadn't happened to be in the shop when it was attacked.

"Italians get prejudice too, you know," Clare told her. "Not as much as blacks, but it still affects you. We get called spics and wops. We get stereotyped. I get really fed up of being cast as a temperamental, busty, dark-haired mediterranean beauty. And they still have fascists in Italy, same as here. It's no good thinking that they'll go away if you ignore them."

On the road where the crowd was gathering, people were handing out "Fight Racism" banners with the Socialist Workers party logo. Ruth didn't take one. That was one reason Ben had given for not going on marches like these, that fringe political groups used them as recruiting grounds and took them over. They had talked quite a lot last night. The more Ruth got to know Ben, the more she liked him. She had to keep reminding herself not to get too involved. But, after last night, it was probably too late.

It was nearly eleven. Ruth guessed that there were about five hundred people there now, as the steward in the black beret made space for the Samba band to get through. The band's leader, a dark-haired young man in sunglasses, blew a whistle and the drums started.

Slowly, the crowd began to take shape and move,

walking across the Forest to Mount Hooton Road. Ruth and Clare were in the middle. As the samba music grew louder and took on a powerful rhythm, they began to move too. The march had begun.

Inspector Grace, in his peaked cap and winter uniform, was ready to supervise the march. Instead, he was listening to Ben. He didn't like what he heard.

"I'm meant to be off today. Instead I find myself having to drum up a few extra officers for this illegal rally. Now you tell me we need CID and the riot squad. If you had this information before, why didn't you reveal it?"

"I got a phone call while I was waiting for the car, sir."

"How do you know it was reliable?"

"I've had contact with the informant on previous occasions, sir."

"I hope you've kept a thorough record of those meetings."

"Yes, sir."

This wasn't strictly true. Ben had taken notes about his off duty meetings with Jed Sutcliffe, but they weren't in his police notebook. Grace shook his head.

"I hate having things suddenly dumped on me."

Then you're in the wrong job, Ben thought. But as he watched Grace make a rapid series of phone calls, his respect for the inspector grew.

"All right," he told Ben five minutes later. "We'd better get over there before they hit the danger zone."

From the car, Grace radioed the sergeant who was currently coordinating the march.

"The front of the march has just reached Waverley Street," Grace was told. "It's all very orderly. No problems."

"Who've you got at the back of the march?" Grace asked.

"I did have one PC on there, sir, but people keep joining. He's nearer the middle now."

"All right," Grace told him. "PC Shipman and I will take the back."

Grace switched the radio off and glanced at Ben.

"You took a beating a couple of weeks ago. Are you fully recovered?"

"Yes, sir."

"We may be vulnerable in this position. If you'd rather…"

Ben shook his head.

"Oh, no, sir. I want to get these bastards. I want it really badly."

Grace nodded.

"Let's hope that CID get here in time to help us arrest them."

They drove past Shakespeare Street, where the Central Police Headquarters was. In an alley opposite, the skinheads waited. Grace glanced at the entrance to the alley and frowned.

"You'd better be right about this," he told Ben, "or we're both going to end up with more than egg on our faces."

They parked the car and walked along one side of the march. Ben looked out for Ruth, but couldn't see her. A light drizzle was falling on the crowd and there were more umbrellas than banners, but the marchers seemed in high spirits.

"Good old Sergeant Rain," Grace said. "He may save the day yet."

Ben couldn't shake the feeling that he should be inside the march with Ruth, not outside, patrolling it. At the front, a small group of percussionists played Latin American music, a loud whistle signalling each tempo change. Each sound of the whistle was like a cry of alarm, Ben thought. It seemed eerily appropriate, as the front of the march turned the corner and strode on to Shakespeare Street.

The demonstrators moved down the hill, past the former polytechnic on one side and the cemetery on the other. As the march progressed, Ruth and Clare dropped towards the back of it. Ruth's legs were short and the pair were engrossed in conversation. Of course, it had proved impossible for Ruth to resist telling Clare about her night with Ben.

"Have you noticed something about this march?" Ruth said to Clare.

"What?"

"It's practically all white."

"They always are," Clare told her. "Guilty white liberals like us. A lot of black people find this kind of thing patronizing."

"You're damned if you do anything and damned if you don't."

"Something like that," Clare said. "Mind you, there's a bloke in a turban back there."

In fact, there were several young Asian men joining the march behind them. They seemed to have emerged from behind the wall in front of the polytechnic building.

"That one looks familiar," Clare said, pointing to a guy in his early twenties. "Isn't he in the job?"

"I don't know," Ruth told her.

Around them, the chanting grew louder and louder.

"We are black. We are white. Together we are dynamite!"

As long as no one starts singing "Ebony and Ivory" I'll be OK, Ruth thought. She wasn't very good at being part of a crowd. She was too much of a loner. But Clare, she noticed, had begun to shout along with the rest. The march had swelled, she realized, as they turned the corner on to Shakespeare Street. There was a different feeling in the air, a kind of excitement.

"This is good," she said to Clare. "I'm enjoying this."

"They get pretty boring after a while," Clare warned her. "Once we get into Market Square, there'll be loads of speeches. We could go shopping though."

"Yeah," said Ruth, "shopping. I like the sound of that."

People began to chant again and this time Ruth joined in.

"Black and white, unite and fight. Smash the BNP!"

The chanting grew louder and louder as the crowd began to march past the Central Police Headquarters. Unnoticed, beside the crowd, a young man wearing braces and a very short haircut was walking rapidly, trying to keep the smug smile off his face.

18

"Not yet, not yet," Brig insisted, as they waited in the alleyway. There were forty-three of them, less than Brig had hoped for, but more than had been on the original bookshop raid. Jed was surprised that so many had shown up. There was a strong likelihood of arrests, yet here, in the alleyway beside the WEA, were some of the legendary figures of modern British fascism: "White" Wally, who claimed to be responsible for harassing over a hundred black families into leaving the Isle of Dogs; Billy "the bigot" Bradshaw, the far right's most prolific graffiti artist; "Mad" Max from Halifax, reputed to have burnt down at least three mosques single-handed, two of them with people inside.

The majority, though, were local. Many of them

had been on the original bookshop raid. A couple were kids who Brig had recruited, with Jed's help, at the youth centre. Jed was sorry about that, but it couldn't be helped. It was their responsibility. True, he had encouraged them to join the party, but they had come to today's terror parade of their own free will.

The scout sidled into the alleyway. He must have looked conspicuous in his braces, Jed thought. Suppose someone had clocked him?

"It couldn't be better," the scout told Brig and the others. "The end of the march is really straggly, and there's a bunch of Pakis in it, too. They should be along in a couple of minutes."

"How many Pakis are there?" Brig asked.

"Ten, fifteen at most, we can take them easily."

"OK." Brig addressed his troops. "We take the Pakis first, the lefties next. Remember, we want to be out in five minutes. You all know where the vans are when we get out of the Victoria Centre. How many police were there?"

"At the back? One or two. There was an inspector for a while, but he seems to have gone."

"I'll look out for him," Brig said.

"And there's this black copper, tall sod."

That must be Ben, Jed thought.

"Jed'll take his radio out like I said, then we'll lay into him first," Brig ordered.

"I can take him on my own," Jed insisted.

Brig shook his head.

"Niggers shouldn't be allowed in the British police force. We'll give him such a hiding that he wants to hand in his badge."

Jed didn't argue. Ben knew what was coming. Hopefully, he was prepared. The scout ducked back down the alley.

"Get ready," he called to the hidden army. "Here they come!"

Ben watched the crowd anxiously. There was no sign of Ruth. But everyone seemed relaxed. They were singing, despite the rain. They wouldn't be, if they knew what Ben knew. Where were the back-ups the inspector had asked for?

As the tail of the march appeared, Ben spotted a few black faces, making him feel less conspicuous. But these were the people who were going to get hit, he realized. At least he had a truncheon to protect himself with. Ben thought back over what Jed had told him. Was it everything, he wondered? If so, why had Jed left it to the last minute to tell him? He must have known that the police would be pushed to organize a response in time.

Suddenly, Ben spotted Ruth. She was with Clare, the two of them singing along happily. He had to get to them, warn them to push their way farther into the crowd. They were too near the back.

Ben pushed into the crowd calling Ruth's name,

but the singing was too loud for her to hear. And there was Inspector Grace, coming towards him. His face looked harassed. He was talking into his radio but broke off as he reached Ben.

"There's been a cock-up. The reinforcements are at the front of the march instead of the back. They've stopped it, so any minute now, there's going to be a bottleneck."

"You mean *here*?" Ben said, trying to keep an eye on Ruth. "But any moment now..."

He couldn't see her any more. The crowd was nearly past the alleyway.

"The back-ups are on their way," Grace told him. "To be honest, I had a hell of a job convincing the Chief Inspector. He wanted to know why we hadn't informed him earlier so that they could round up the skinheads and put them behind bars until this was over. Are you sure they're really there?"

Ben looked over the inspector's shoulder and braced himself for action.

"I'm very sure, sir," he said. "Just look behind you."

Suddenly, the singing stopped. For a moment, Ruth didn't register what was going on. But then Clare swore, something she didn't normally do, and Ruth turned round. A swarm of short-haired, short-necked men in blue denim were charging into the crowd, fists flailing. A few of them carried large pieces of wood. Ruth saw at least one with a knife.

In front of her, someone began to scream. There was a stampede. But the fascists weren't chasing the women and children, who were running away towards the Victoria Centre. They were laying into the Asian men who had joined the back end of the march.

She saw skinheads she recognized. One was the man she had followed to the youth centre. He was grabbing a police officer, an inspector by the look of it, tearing off his radio. And the other man she recognized was Jed Sutcliffe. He was running towards another police officer – she could only see the uniform – with a knife in his hand. Instinctively, Ruth pushed towards the officer in danger.

"My God," Clare said, pushing after her. "Do you see who that is?"

Ruth wasn't tall enough to see the officer's face. Only patches of uniform showed through the crowd.

"No," she said to her friend. "Who?"

Clare pulled Ruth through the fighting crowd. Any moment now, one of them was going to get hit. The police officer had probably been stabbed already. A horrible thought struck Ruth.

"It's not Neil, is it?" she asked Clare.

"No," Clare replied. "I'm afraid it's Ben."

Jed pushed his way towards Ben Shipman. *Where are they?* he kept asking himself, *Where are they?* There weren't even any back-up police officers. If Ben had been home last night, he'd have had the information in time to use it properly. He reached Ben a few metres ahead of Mad Max, who also wanted a piece of the policeman. Jed held up his knife to Ben.

"Quick!" he said. "Pretend to take this off me."

Ben grabbed Jed's lower arm with his left hand, then pretended to grapple for the knife with his right.

"I thought you might have brought your own troops," he said to Jed.

"So did I," Jed told him. "But where are yours?"

"They're on their way."

"Good," said Jed, "so am I. Look out behind you."

He ran towards the pub on the corner, where a photographer was supposed to be waiting. Jed could tell him which mugs to snap. Ben Shipman, meanwhile, would have to look after himself.

Ben looked around. The first thing he saw was Ruth, running towards him. Clare Coppola followed, a couple of feet behind. She was pointing. The next thing he saw was a big bus with shaded windows, moving across the street to block it. It must be one of those coach parties, on its way to the Royal Concert Hall for a matinée. Normally, they could drive along here, but it should have been diverted because of the march. Now it was blocking the back-up police officers' approach.

Then he saw what Ruth was pointing at: a fierce-looking, gigantic skinhead with bloodshot eyes, waving a crowbar. A knife would be no match for an attack from that. Ben dropped the knife and pulled out his truncheon, knowing that that would be no use either. He ought to run. But how could he run when Clare and Ruth were on their way to help him? How could he look like a coward in front of her? He hesitated, fatally. The large skinhead swung the crowbar at him.

Ruth watched as Ben ducked the blow, then she did the only thing which she could think of. She dived at the skinhead's feet. The rugby tackle worked. The skinhead lost his balance and, before he could regain it, Clare and Ben charged him, knocking him to the ground. Clare held him down as Ben restrained him with handcuffs. Pulling herself from the ground, Ruth looked around to see if anyone else was coming after the three of them. She got a shock.

A bus had parked in the middle of Shakespeare Street, blocking the road in front of the Central Police Station. Out of the bus charged a crowd of stick-wielding men, but these ones did not have tattoos or short hair. There were as many blacks as there were whites, and they were laying into the racists with everything they had. From the pavement, bystanders stared in horror. They must think that they'd been transported to a war zone.

As Ruth watched, several of the fascists saw that they were hopelessly outnumbered. They began to run up the street, towards the Victoria Centre. But their timing couldn't have been worse. As they hurried past the bus, the skinheads ran into a phalanx of uniformed police officers, their truncheons raised. The skinheads turned back again, only to face a huge crowd of anti-racists. Sheepishly, pathetically, they turned back again and began surrendering to the police.

"Get that one, and that one. See the one with the red shirt over there. Don't miss him."

Jed was making sure that all of the important Nazis on the march were photographed. As he watched, the boys arrived, better late than never. They were all anti-Nazi activists who weren't afraid to use violence. A friend of a friend had rung round the night before to round them up. But even with them here, some of the fascists were bound to get away. Jed wanted them photographed before that happened.

"Him, over there! Take him before he gets away."

The one running was Brig. He had seen how the land lay and was getting out. Instead of running towards the Victoria Centre, as was the plan, he was running back the way the march had come. Jed looked down the street, saw the police, and realized why Brig had gone the way he had.

"Did you get him?"

The photographer shook his head.

"Next time."

"If that guy comes across me again," Jed told him, "I won't be alive next time."

"This is turning into a riot," Ben told Ruth after he had thanked her and Clare for helping him.

"More like a war," Clare corrected him.

"At least the right side are winning," Ruth said. "They're getting what they had coming to them."

"Violence is never the right answer," Ben told her, as they watched another skinhead getting his head kicked in by three whites and one Asian. "Martin Luther King said…"

"Never mind what Martin Luther King said," Ruth interrupted. "There's the one you were after, up the hill there, in the red shirt. He's getting away!"

All three of them gave chase, but Ben was faster, and soon got ahead of Ruth and Clare. At first, Ben's chest hurt him, and he thought that he wasn't up to it. Then he recovered his rhythm. He had his health back. The skinhead, who Jed said was called Brig, crossed over Waverley Street and headed up the hill, out of sight.

Ben picked up pace. He didn't know what he'd do if he caught Brig. He'd used his handcuffs on the skinhead who'd attacked him. He'd lost his truncheon in the melée below. But he'd deal with that when he got there. Turning the corner, he saw Brig crossing the road and charging into the cemetery. Ben would have to catch him before he got out the other side. Otherwise the skinhead could jump on one of a hundred buses on the Derby Road and disappear for ever.

There were only two ways you could go when you got to the cemetery: uphill or along the side. Ben hurried uphill, hoping that Brig had worked out that this was the best way out. He could hear Brig's rapid footsteps ahead of him. He could hear other footsteps, presumably Ruth and Clare. He didn't have time to look back. In fact, there seemed to be altogether too many footsteps.

Then they stopped.

There was a clearing in the centre of the cemetery. In the middle of it was a pile of dead wood, waiting to be chopped up. From behind the pile of wood came an anguished yelling. Panting, out of breath, Ben stopped to take in the scene he found there.

Brig lay on the floor. His arms were twisted. Blood poured from his head. There were five Asian men around him. None were armed, although the wood next to them would have made an excellent weapon. They had done enough damage without it.

Ben radioed for an ambulance.

Four of the Asian men ran off. The fifth stood facing Ben. It was Baljit.

"Am I under arrest?" he asked.

"You're not," Ben said. "He is. Now get out of here quickly, before someone else arrives."

19

The police press conference was brief and to the point. Ruth was impressed by the way Inspector Grace handled it. His arm was in a sling from when he'd been attacked by Brig.

"Acting on information received, I called for uniformed back-up and CID involvement. The uniforms arrived with commendable speed, in time to arrest large numbers of offenders, forty-four in all."

"How many were fascists and how many were anti-fascists?" the stringer for the *Guardian* wanted to know.

"I'm not in a position to state the political opinions of the offenders. However, thirty-six of those arrested had very short haircuts."

There was an appreciative laugh from the journalists.

"What charges are being brought?"

"I can't be too specific about that. The charges are likely to range from affray to actual bodily harm. Some of those arrested are also being questioned about earlier offences which they may have committed."

"Can you tell us who the police informant was, Inspector Grace?"

"I'm afraid that our policy is to protect our sources for…"

"Is it the skinhead mole who's giving a press conference for *Searchlight* across the road in five minutes?"

"I know nothing about…"

Inspector Grace looked discomfited. Ben, who was standing next to Ruth, murmured, "I'll catch you later" and slipped out of the building. The reporter from the *Evening Post* was saying:

"Isn't it the case that this march should never have been allowed to go ahead at such short notice? The law clearly states—"

Grace interrupted him.

"The march organizers cooperated with the police. The attack which took place could have happened even if the statutory period of notice had been given. What we had today were two groups of people bent on violence."

The *Guardian* stringer called out,

"Are you criticizing the anti-Nazi activists? Most reports indicated that their arrival stopped the Nazis doing severe harm to peaceful demonstrators."

"Doubtless," Grace said testily, "the anti-Nazis who arrived on the bus will portray themselves as the cavalry arriving to save the day. You will understand if I do not share that view, especially since at least two of them assaulted police officers who were trying to prevent further violence."

Suddenly, the questions dried up. The dozen journalists began to move away. The two TV crews were pushing their way out. Grace looked bewildered. He had been upstaged. Ruth followed the journalists as they hurried towards the pub across the road.

"Don't you think it might be wise to hold on?" Ben asked Jed.

"Why? We want to make the Sunday papers."

"Some of the stuff you told me, it affects ongoing police investigations. You're not going to mention anything about the cash cards, are you?"

Jed's minder leant over. Ben wasn't sure precisely which group he represented.

"Exposure's the best way to deal with these people, officer," he said.

"No," said Ben, "a court of law's the best place to

deal with *these people*, same as any other people. And for that you need proof, carefully put together evidence."

"I'm sorry," Jed said, "but this is my show, not yours. I can't wait that long."

It was no use. The youth was set on saying whatever he had to say. And Ben had to admit that, without him, the march might have had a much unhappier ending. He spotted Ruth in the crowd pressing into the small pub room and joined her. At the front of the now crowded room, the minder began to speak.

"For the last six months, Jed Sutcliffe has been working as a mole reporting for *Searchlight*, getting as close as possible to the command structures of racist groups operating in England today. This morning, as a result of his activities, several prominent racists have been arrested and are likely to be imprisoned for a long time. But that's not the most sensational aspect of this story. I give you … Jed Sutcliffe."

Jed spoke modestly. The yobbish sneer had gone out of his voice, but his accent was still recognizably Mansfield.

"I left school last summer," he said. "That was when I first became aware that racist groups were actively recruiting in the area where I live. It made me angry. One of my best mates at school was black. At least he was my best mate until his family moved because they were sick of having petrol poured through their letterbox. I wanted to do something about it. No one asked me to be a mole. I wrote to *Searchlight* and they said that I was too young to do what I wanted to do, that it was too dangerous. But when it became clear that I was doing it anyway, various anti-racists gave me information, let me know who they were after.

"I found out more than I bargained for. At first, my aim was to expose the racists' methods and maybe get evidence against individuals. I wanted to put people like Richard Brignall and 'White' Wally Marshall in prison. But I also wanted to find out who funded the racists. *Searchlight* assumed that it was European fascist groups siphoning EC funds to English groups. However, I found that the money men were much closer to home…"

He held up a fistful of white plastic cards with laminated strips across them.

"These are cash cards which can only have been produced with the cooperation of the banks whose machines they work in. I received these cards from Richard Brignall two weeks ago. I have taped evidence which shows that the person behind this fraud, which probably involves hundreds of thousands of pounds, is a Nottingham lawyer by the name of Ian Jagger…"

Ruth glanced up at Ben.

"Is it true?" she asked him.

"It's what Jed told me on the phone this morning. But whether he can prove it…"

Now Jed was drowned in a flood of questions.

"Were you involved in the mosque attack last weekend?"

"Have you been involved in any other acts of violence for which you yourself could be arrested?"

"Couldn't you have stopped the riot this morning if you'd informed the police earlier?"

Patiently, Jed answered them all. He had, he admitted, been involved in the attack on the mosque. In fact, he had set Kirk Hepton up. His captors had allowed Jed to escape. There were three other occasions where he got involved in violent acts. One was the attack on the bookshop, for which he had been cautioned. Another was in a newsagent in Mansfield, where the owner was not pressing charges. The third was an assault on a black police officer, which he couldn't have prevented without exposing himself. He had, however, called the police himself as soon as the attackers left. In each of these cases, he was proving himself to the fascist group he was infiltrating and regretted the damage done.

"What about these allegations against Ian Jagger?" the man from the *Evening Post* wanted to know. "He's one of the most respected lawyers in the area. You can't expect us to print these stories unless you have substantial proof."

"I have plenty of proof," Jed said. "You'll forgive

me if I give it to the police first, rather than you."

"What does he have?" Ruth asked Ben.

"There's a tape recording of Brig giving him the cards. I don't know how much it implicates Jagger. CID will be interviewing Brig as soon as the doctors'll let them."

After a few more minutes, the conference broke up. Ben noticed that Inspector Grace was standing in the doorway, along with Detective Inspector Greasby. As the press left, the two men went up to Jed.

"We'd like you to come with us, please, to assist us with our enquiries."

Jed stood and grinned like a cheeky schoolboy who'd just put one over on his teacher.

"My pleasure, gentlemen."

As they left, Ben put his arm around Ruth.

"Come on," he told her. "Let's salvage what we can of the weekend."

It was ten in the morning before Ruth went down to pick up the milk from Ben's doorstep. It turned out that he had a paper delivered too. She took the *Independent on Sunday* upstairs to read it while she was making a pot of tea. Then she took the paper and the teapot into the bedroom and woke him up.

"Look who made the front page."

He kissed her forehead. Then, he sleepily slurped from his mug of tea while reading the article. The confrontation got ten column inches but no photograph:

A continuing wave of racist violence continues to spread across the country with major incidents in Lewisham, Derby, Birmingham and Liverpool yesterday. But in Nottingham, the tide turned for the racists, when a combination of police and anti-Nazi activists stopped a violent attempt to break up a demonstration. There were forty-four arrests, the vast majority being members of fascist organisations, including several notorious..."

"Is there nothing about Jagger?" Ben asked.
"Nothing."
"What about Jed?"
"Last paragraph."

The intelligence which allowed yesterday's successful counter-attack was obtained by a seventeen-year-old anti-racist "mole" who infiltrated the racists' East Midlands recruitment campaign. "It wasn't difficult," said the youth, who cannot be named for his own safety. "Most of these idiots are as thick as two short planks. But there are powerful people behind them." The youth has made several allegations which are the subject of an ongoing police investigation.

"Do you think they'll get Jagger?" Ruth asked, when he'd finished reading.

"Your guess is as good as mine. Probably better. You've met Jagger, haven't you?"

"I have," Ruth admitted. "He's so slimy he could slip away from anything."

"Well, there's your answer."

Ben drained his tea, threw the paper aside and got out of bed.

"I'll just take a quick shower," he told her. "Join me if you like."

"In a minute or two."

Ruth finished her tea and tried to concentrate on an article about arming the police. But it was impossible. She was too happy. If someone had told her that she would spend practically the whole weekend with Ben, that they would be as close as this so soon, she would have laughed in their face.

In the next room, the phone rang.

"Shall I get that?" she called through to the shower.

No reply. What the heck. She went through to the living-room and picked it up. A familiar voice spoke at the other end.

"Hello sweetie. I catch you in at last."

Ruth said nothing.

"Look, I've got to come to Nottingham sooner than I thought. Today, in fact. I was wondering if you could meet me at the station. Ben…? Ben?"

"I'm sorry," Ruth said. "I think you have the wrong number."

She put the phone down.

Ben was singing in the shower. Ruth pulled the cubicle door open.

"You can't come in like that," he told her. "Or were you planning on getting my favourite shirt wet?"

From the next room, the phone began to ring again.

"That'll be Charlene," Ruth told him. "She's coming to Nottingham today and wants you to meet her at the station."

His face fell.

"Oh. What did you…?"

"It's all right. I told her she had a wrong number."

She half turned.

"I'm going now. Remember what we said. No strings."

She didn't wait for Ben to reply. In the bedroom, she dressed hurriedly, hoping that he wouldn't answer the phone. But he did. It was almost too much to bear; his tender voice talking to another woman, one who had far greater claims on him than she could ever have. Ruth found her car keys and slipped out of the flat quietly, without saying good-bye.

EPILOGUE

"I've made a decision," Neil told Ben at the start of the shift.

"Don't tell me," Ben said. "You put in for that attachment to CID."

Neil nodded.

"You don't mind, do you?"

Ben smiled ruefully and tried to make light of it.

"Losing my tutor officer? Why should I mind? I've already lost one. I've learned everything I could learn from you anyway."

Neil laughed.

"The thing is, I really fancy the job. And I don't want to work on the same shift as Clare again. It's too much pressure."

"I can understand that," Ben told him.

"We'll be neighbours, though," Neil added. "We'll still be mates, right?" Neil held out his hand. Ben shook it, firmly.

"Right."

Inspector Grace walked through to his office. He greeted Ben and Neil.

"Did you hear about Richard Brignall?"

Ben shook his head.

"He's out on bail already and alleging police brutality."

"That's not what happened," Ben told the inspector.

Grace looked around. They were the only three people in the parade room.

"Between us three, no one would blame you if you had given him that kicking. Just stick to your story. He hasn't got a chance."

The inspector left. Ben sighed and continued filling in his notebook. Neil typed out an arrest report.

"Have you seen this?"

Both men turned round. Standing in the doorway to the parade room was Jed Sutcliffe. He was holding a copy of that day's *Evening Post*.

"What's it about?" Ben asked.

"Jagger."

Ben was surprised that the local paper had done a story on the allegations against Jagger. None of the nationals had touched it. But the page five article wasn't about Jed's allegations. It was a brief puff piece, accompanying a photograph.

Newly-qualified solicitor Charlene Harris is the latest addition to popular local law firm, Jagger and partners. Ms Harris, 23, told the Post that she's very happy to be coming to Nottingham for "personal reasons". "It's a very exciting city which I know well," she said. Senior partner, Ian Jagger, pictured here with his newest recruit, said that Ms Harris will specialize in crime work.

The picture showed a smiling Charlene shaking hands with Jagger.

"He's a racist!" Jed protested. "He's hired a black lawyer as a front. And this isn't a news story. The front page story doesn't mention Jagger, or me. The paper have printed it as a way of showing anyone who heard them that the allegations I made against him are false!"

"I'm afraid you're right," Ben said.

"What I'd like to know," Jed went on, "is what kind of woman would work for a guy like him."

"I expect that Jagger convinced her she was chosen on merit," Neil said, tactfully.

"Then she's kidding herself."

Ben said nothing.

"I think Inspector Grace is waiting to see you," Neil told Jed. "You'd better go through."

When Jed had gone, the two men looked at each other.

"Did you know this?" Neil asked.

Ben shook his head.

"Have you seen her?"

Again, Ben shook his head. Since the weekend, he had put Charlene off, told her that he had other commitments, that he had to think about things. He hadn't even asked about her new job. He wished he had. He could have warned her what she'd be getting herself into.

Charlene had probably guessed that he'd been seeing someone else. He guessed she'd been seeing other men, too, but casually, the way he'd meant to keep it with Ruth. If Ben saw Charlene now, he knew, he would be seduced. He would let her move in. But he wasn't sure if that was what he really wanted, any more. He needed time to make up his mind. When he got off the phone, Ruth was gone. And he hadn't had the nerve to call her, either. Because that might have committed him to her, and he wasn't sure whether he wanted that, either.

A phone rang. Neil answered it.

"Speak of the devil," he said. "I've just been looking at your picture in the paper."

Ben gave an exasperated sigh. Neil glanced at him and he shook his head.

"He's not here I'm afraid," Neil told Charlene. "He's on patrol. Yes, I should have been with him but I've been in court all morning. Yes, I'll tell him. 'Bye."

"Thanks," Ben told Neil when he'd put the phone down.

"You'd do the same for me. But you won't be able to hold her off for long, you know. She's a persistent woman. And now she knows what shift you're on."

It was true, Ben realized. Even if he went to his parents, she would find him quickly enough. He would have to see her, tonight. He would have to warn her about Jagger. Would she believe him, or think it was sour grapes, designed to get her away from Nottingham? Should he tell her about Ruth? He would have to decide.

"Why haven't they printed it?" Jed wanted to know. "We got him, didn't we?"

"You may have *got him*," the smooth inspector said, "but no paper is likely to print the story unless he's charged. They don't print that kind of story about a lawyer unless they're on very sure ground."

"But the tape…"

"The tape seems to imply that Mr Jagger was involved in supplying dubious cash cards, but Richard Brignall denies this. He says he was winding you up…"

"That's rubbish."

"Maybe. But these are powerful people you're talking about. Brignall claims to have got the cards from someone with fascist connections who works in the bank's computer section. There's nothing to link Jagger in at all. You've sown a few seeds of doubt in people's minds, but you've probably blown the police investigation. Now that the allegations are out in the open, anyone involved in the fraud will have covered their tracks."

"I don't believe it," Jed protested. "You're wrong."

"It's not me saying this," Grace told him. "It's CID. Anyway, you should count your lucky stars. If you were legally an adult, Jagger could sue you for slander. He'd almost certainly win."

"Win what? All I've got is the clothes I stand up in."

Grace smiled sympathetically.

"I don't know whether I believe your story or not. The fact that the man defends racist thugs doesn't make him one. And as for the bank card thing – that would strain anyone's credulity. But you got a result yesterday. In my book, you're a hero."

Jed blinked.

"You mean that?"

The inspector's smile became diplomatic.

"I'm speaking off the record, of course. No one condones violence, but the right people got hurt for a change. Now, on the record, I hope you've got somewhere to hide for a few months."

Jed nodded.

"I'm going to write the story of how I did it. There's this bloke in…"

Grace shushed him.

"Don't tell me. I don't want to know. Just make sure we have a way of contacting you when you have to appear in court. And don't worry, when that happens, you'll be protected."

Protected from who? Jed wondered. From Brig, when he got out of prison? From Jagger? From any neo-Nazi with half a brain who happened to fancy his chances? Grace went on.

"When the court appearances are over, grow your hair, change as much as you can about your appearance. But not until all the appearances are over or you'll be even more vulnerable. We'll tell you when."

On the way out, Jed saw Ben again. The police officer still had the photograph from the *Post* in front of him. He looked very fed up.

"You should have told me earlier," Ben said, as Jed greeted him. "We could have stopped the violence. It would have been a successful march, an effective protest. As it was, all people will remember is the fighting. Violence solves nothing. You set a bad example."

"Maybe," Jed said. "We'll have to agree to disagree on that one."

"You set them up," Ben told him.

"Yeah," Jed smiled. "Sweet, wasn't it?"

He offered Ben his hand. The police officer thought for a moment, then shook it.

"That thing with Jagger," Jed said, as they parted. "I blew it."

Ben shrugged.

"If he's bent, we'll get him in the end."

Jed shook his head. Behind him, the inspector came out of his office.

"You'd better keep your eye on this one," Jed told Grace. "I think he's an idealist."

Out on the street, Jed kept looking around him. Then his minder drove alongside. Jed got into the car and they drove off. Jed slumped in the seat, keeping his head down. He would not see the city again until he went to court. How long would it be before he could go home? He knew the answer to that one. Never.

Jed found himself thinking about that Indian guy, the one who wrote a novel and ended up with a *fatwa* – a death sentence which would hang over him for the rest of his life. Jed had an idea of how that guy must feel.

But Jed had chosen this situation himself. He'd known what he was getting into. They would be after him, yes, and he would take precautions. But he wouldn't spend his whole life in hiding, because, if he did, they'd have won. The inspector had called Jed a hero. But Jed didn't feel like a hero. He didn't feel any different. No, that wasn't true. For the first time since this started, Jed felt afraid. This wasn't an exciting adventure any more.

And it was only just beginning.

Look out for the next exciting
instalment from

in
Smokescreen

The call came in at ten past midnight.

"Fire reported at Greencoat School."

Jan answered, "4523 responding. Any further information available?"

"Caller reports smoke rising from school site. That's all."

"Probably some kids set fire to a bin," Clare commented.

"Let's hope so," Jan said.

Clare put the flashing light on and accelerated towards the ring road.

"Greencoat's your old school, isn't it?" Jan asked.

"That's right," Clare told her. "Seems a long time ago."

But it wasn't, Jan thought, not really. Only four and a bit years had passed since Clare left school, went to sixth form college, then on to university. Only a few months ago, Clare dropped out of university and joined the police force.

"It's not a bin," Jan said, as they turned off the ring road and approached the school. Massive flames licked the roof of one of the buildings, illuminating the night sky.

"Here we go," Jan muttered, as a fire engine, siren blaring, followed them into the car park. "Looks like it's starting all over again."

The night shift was barely two hours old. So far, Jan and Clare had visited three public houses, to make sure that they were throwing drinkers out on time; they had broken up a loud domestic argument between a husband and wife, both drunk, without an arrest; they had stopped a Fiesta with a broken tail light and cautioned the driver; and they'd nearly run over a cyclist with no lights. When Jan asked the cyclist if he was trying to commit suicide, the youth told her where to go and what to do there. But they let him off anyway. The offence wasn't worth the paperwork which went with it.

A minute ago, Clare had felt like falling asleep. Now, as she got out of the car, her pulse raced. This was police work: hours of boredom followed by sudden fear and exhilaration. Clare had never been to a big fire before.

While Jan called the fire in to the CID Night

Crime Patrol, Clare got as close to the blaze as she dared. She guided the firefighters through the maze of buildings to the centre, where the flames were. The building on fire was the main hall, which doubled as the school's theatre. At the back of the hall, Clare knew, the school stored countless old wooden desks, which were used for exams, or as drama props.

The heat from the hall was overpowering. On stage, the vast red curtains were ablaze. Burning fabric cascaded on to the chairs where Clare used to sit in assemblies, bored out of her skull. She could see the wooden desks now, going up in flames like a funeral pyre. Clare squinted, trying to make out any signs of what had started the fire, before the flames destroyed the evidence along with the school.

"Are you mad?" a firefighter yelled, pushing her aside. "Get out of here now! This area's dangerous."

Clare felt foolish. At any moment, bits of burning building could fall on her. The firefighters, unlike Clare, wore protective clothing. She ran back to the shelter of the administration block, where Jan was standing with a sour-faced man who Clare recognized as the caretaker.

"I checked it before locking up. It's not down to me."

"Could someone have hidden in there, perhaps?" Jan asked, tactfully.

"Under the stage, I suppose. I don't look there."

"You don't live on the site?"

"Just down the road. I came out when I heard the sirens."

"What about the smoke alarms? Didn't they sound?"

"You can only hear them properly when you're inside the building."

"Are CID on their way?" Clare interrupted.

Jan frowned.

"Duty Officer's in Hucknall, so it'll be a while. We're to keep the scene secure."

After midnight, there was only one CID officer and an assistant on duty to cover four divisions. One detective covered Hucknall, Radford Road, Arnold and Carlton.

"I'll take a look around," Clare told Jan. "See if I can work out how they got in."

Jan nodded and started questioning the caretaker again. Clare walked round the administration building, taking the long route so that she could get safely to the other side of the hall, which connected with one of the main teaching blocks. She'd known that CID would be called in: they always were when serious arson was suspected. But she was glad that they would be a while. Clare liked the opportunity to do her own detective work.

This was the first major school fire of the year, but it wouldn't be the last. The year before, arson spread across the city's schools like an infectious disease. In one case, a couple of young men stole a car and smashed it into a classroom. Then they set the car alight, burning down half the school. In another incident, a school hall was set on fire in the lunch hour, minutes before a hundred and fifty twelve-year-olds went to register there.

The arsonists, Clare knew, were usually connected with the school. Also, they liked to watch. Clare could understand why. The fire raged in the night sky. Even at this distance, the heat was uncomfortably strong. Clare ought to be angry: this was her old school burning down. But she was also impressed. The fire had a savage, primordial power. It was hard not to stare. Was someone else watching with the same feelings – watching with pride, because they started it?

Where would Clare watch from if she'd started the fire? Clare thought for a moment, then hurried to the back of the school, towards the playing field. She studied a distant bank of grass, which backed on to an estate of council houses.

In her dark uniform, Clare didn't expect to be seen. It was a clear night, and she could make out the silhouette of someone standing on the bank, beside a beech tree.

At the same moment, the watcher spotted Clare. He or she turned and began to run away from the school. Clare gave chase.

Other books by David Belbin in

P●INT CRiME

AVENGING ANGEL

Traffic's murder tonight…

Clare and Neil of The Beat meet as they
investigate Clare's brother's death…

BREAK POINT

Game, set and … murder…

FINAL CUT

Lights, camera … murder…

SHOOT THE TEACHER

Even teachers don't deserve to die…